PENGUIN
MAKING THE MI

Anurag Mathur was born in Delhi and educated at Scindia School, Gwalior, St. Stephen's College, Delhi and the University of Tulsa, Oklahoma, USA. He is a journalist in the print and electronic media and loves music, eating out and tennis—besides reading, of course. His published books include the best-selling novels *The Inscrutable Americans* and *Scenes from an Executive Life*.

MAKING THE MINISTER SMILE

Anurag Mathur

PENGUIN BOOKS

PENGUIN BOOKS
Published by the Penguin Group
Penguin Books India Pvt Ltd, 11 Community Centre, Panchsheel Park, New Delhi 110 017, India
Penguin Group (USA) Inc., 375 Hudson Street, New York, New York 10014, USA
Penguin Group (Canada), 90 Eglinton Avenue East, Suite 700, Toronto, Ontario, M4P 2Y3, Canada (a division of Pearson Penguin Canada Inc.)
Penguin Books Ltd, 80 Strand, London WC2R 0RL, England
Penguin Ireland, 25 St Stephen's Green, Dublin 2, Ireland (a division of Penguin Books Ltd)
Penguin Group (Australia), 250 Camberwell Road, Camberwell, Victoria 3124, Australia (a division of Pearson Australia Group Pty Ltd)
Penguin Group (NZ), cnr Airborne and Rosedale Roads, Albany, Auckland 1310, New Zealand (a division of Pearson New Zealand Ltd)
Penguin Group (South Africa) (Pty) Ltd, 24 Sturdee Avenue, Rosebank, Johannesburg 2196, South Africa

Penguin Books Ltd, Registered Offices: 80 Strand, London WC2R 0RL, England

First published by A'N'B Publishers Pvt Ltd, New Delhi 1996
Published by Penguin Books India 2002

Copyright © Anurag Mathur 1996

10 9 8

This is a work of fiction. Names, characters, places and incidents are either the product of the author's imagination or are used fictitiously, and any resemblance to any actual person, living or dead, events or locales is entirely coincidental.

For sale in the Indian Subcontinent and Singapore only

Printed at Pauls Press, New Delhi

This book is dedicated to my sister, Sujata

1

"Jeez," grumbled Chris to himself and not for the first time, "this country just ain't built for football players." He twisted awkwardly on the bed as his feet stuck out over the edge. In the distance he heard a loud voice.

"Why you are damn fooling me, I say?" demanded Mr. Sunder irately. "Why you are teasing, torturing and befooling me?"

Mr. Sunder was annoyed. His displeasure, apparently being expressed over the telephone in the verandah, wafted into Chris's bedroom, waking him as he was dozing off. Chris grinned sleepily, extremely amused as always at Mr. Sunder's earnestness, pomposity and unique version of the English language. He stretched his 6ft 4in, 300lbs football players' frame.

It was a glorious winter afternoon in New Delhi. 'What more can anyone ask for?' drowsily thought Chris, gazing contentedly out of the window. 'Green grass, blooming flowers, gentle sunshine and Mr. Sunder speaking English on the verandah.'

"You scoundrel," screamed Mr. Sunder, "You dirty rogue. You bloody nonsense fellow." Words apparently failed Mr. Sunder now as the phone was slammed back.

'Ouch,' winced Chris. He wondered what had disturbed Mr. Sunder so deeply. Perhaps a potato had been found to be rotten. Or a tomato to be pulpy. Or perhaps even, horrors, the meat to be a day old. Such events, Chris had found during his month-old stay in Delhi in the Kapoors' house, profoundly distressed Mr. Sunder.

Mr. Sunder was the presiding deity of the Kapoor household. Though his formal designation was merely Assistant Manager (Administration) in KapCo Ltd. (making First Class Utensils For First Class People), it failed to hint at the profound importance of his job. It was his responsibility, perhaps even, his demeanour suggested, his divinely commanded duty, to ensure that all went well in the home inhabited by Ram Avtar Kapoor, the Kap in KapCo, and his son, Ajai Vir.

It was not a small role, felt Mr. Sunder, and he never let anyone forget it. He fascinated Chris. And the fascination, truth to tell, was mutual. Since neither of the Kapoors ever paid the slightest attention to Mr. Sunder, for him to find a guest like Chris from distant America being courteous and thankful for his services, drove Mr. Sunder into a frenzy of subservience.

When Chris continued to be kind, this was not unmixed with a certain sense of mystification at all the attention. Chris didn't think he had been particularly attentive, but perhaps, he thought, he had, when compared to the Kapoor father and son who, despite having enjoyed Mr. Sunder's devotions for the last eleven years, frequently forgot his name.

Mr. Sunder had brooded about Chris's courtesy for some time and had come to a conclusion.

"I think," he had informed Chris knowingly quite recently, "you are accepting me as your guru about India".

No number of subtle hints and more pointed denials had been able to dissuade him and he had begun offering original interpretations regarding the mysteries of India to Chris. Lately he had started adding his views on western

2

civilisation as well as his suggestions for improving it. Of course, as he was the first to point out, he had never actually visited any of the western countries, or indeed any country outside India, but such a shortcoming, he felt, had the charm of enhancing his objectivity.

Chris wondered hopefully if Mr. Sunder was coming across to offer some fresh views, but his footsteps dwindled away. He stretched, thinking of how he came to be here and his experiences in the last month.

It had all been quite sudden. His father owned Stark Plastics, a small but highly-regarded company making plastic products, and when he came home after his final semester in college he was told of the exciting new collaboration between them and KapCo in India who wanted to diversify from steel into plastics. The project progressed smoothly, with executives from India coming to be trained and orders being placed for the appropriate injection machines and moulds to be sent to India.

Then suddenly there had been a silence. When Chris, who had become interested in the project as soon as he had started working for his father, faxed to ask the reason, he received an unsatisfactory reply about 'Labour problems'.

"May be I can help explain what its all about and try and sort it out", he suggested to his father.

"Sure," the old man had grunted. "With your vast experience of six months."

But he had let him go. A letter to the Kapoors had elicited a cordial invitation to stay with them, which Chris had accepted with unseemly haste. He prepared in a blur of packing, visas, and sage counsel. 'Don't drink the water.' And had arrived one chilly and misty dawn at Indira Gandhi International Airport outside Delhi.

He was groggy from the 19 hour flight from New York with a bare one hour stopover in London. He wasn't sure what time it was in Delhi but it was dark outside the aircraft. He shuffled through the door and into a large hall that looked like every arrival area in the world. An anxious look around showed that there were no starving millions waving pitiful stumps and begging for alms and American visas.

Chris recognised that this was an unreasonable fear, but he had heard so much about the poverty that he had actually half feared some sort of heart rending reception. Now he stood patiently in line as an extremely fat and bad-tempered looking man sitting behind a counter irately surveyed proferred passports as though it was the very last thing he wanted to do.

When Chris reached him, the man coughed gratingly, gargled loudly and spat a thick wad of blood into a bin. Chris recoiled. 'Shit' he thought, 'the guy's got tuberculosis.' He tried not to breathe. 'Jesus, fifteen minutes in India and I'm going to be infected with TB,' he thought, holding himself rigid.

The man looked at him evilly. He pawed greedily through the passport as though hoping to find pornographic pictures printed in it. Finally he gave up in disgust, stamped something on a vacant page and hawked another stream of blood into a spitoon.

Shaken, Chris scampered through, finally allowing himself to breathe. 'How does he look so healthy with his lungs all gone?' he wondered. 'And why do they let him work in a place where he can infect half the people visiting India? Helluva welcome. But then maybe,' he thought, calming down, 'the guy is probably the only breadwinner in the family and needs to work. I mean he can't enjoy being up all night working when he's coughing his guts out?'

4

And so, wondering about the man, sorry for him, yet concerned about his own susceptibility to infection, he went through the motions of collecting his baggage and going through the green channel.

'I wonder if I can get some kind of shots to stop TB before it develops in me,' he worried. 'Shit. I hope I wasn't wrong in coming here. I hope I get back alive'.

Distractedly he wheeled his cart through an open door and a vast crowd pounced on him. They were all around, yelling, waving, beckoning.

'The starving millions,' Chris thought numbly, 'so I really was right'.

Then he noticed they were held back by a barrier and were screaming things like 'Taxi', "You come here only," and one was actually whistling at him. Amidst the convulsing throng he saw a sign bobbing that said 'Chris Stark' and headed for it.

The taxi drivers in that section seemed delirious that he had chosen their part of the crowd and swarmed around him in ecstasy. Someone tried to help him push the cart, another pulled his sleeve, one seemed to have become permanently gummed to his coat, two others were clawing each other seeking his patronage and a turbaned gentleman was hissing things into his ear that Chris couldn't understand, but whose meaning was universal. He found time to wonder, even in the frenzy, whether an ungodly hour of the night, to a jet lagged and irritable passenger was the best time and place to offer unspeakable oriental delights and whether the turbaned guy got many ... or for that matter any ... acceptances.

Then there was a shout, irate words from a tall, slender young man who scattered the crowd. A few tenacious types remained, apparently so enamoured of Chris even in this brief meeting that they were refusing to be parted. They looked beseechingly at him and Chris could have sworn their eyes shone with unshed tears. Hardening his heart to them, he greeted his rescuer.

"You must be Ajai," said Chris shaking hands with the bespectacled Indian.

"Right. Sorry about all this, but its our traditional welcome to India. Lets go this way."

As Chris accompanied Ajai he noticed one of his bags was missing: Throughout his trip he was be to amazed at the strange behaviour of luggage. All his life in America he had found that bags were just bags. They lay there, you filled them up with things and then you carried them about wherever you went. If you put them somewhere they stayed put. They were peaceful if inanimate companions. But in India, they miraculously came to life, taking on the magic, mystery and personality of frisky elves.

How else could you explain a suitcase secured in a cart suddenly vanishing? In later months he was to observe even more perplexing behaviour. A bag that was at his side seconds ago would suddenly be glimpsed on the head of a coolie striding determinedly out of the Railway Station. A suitcase secure inside a hotel room cupboard would appear tied with ropes to the roof of a taxi parked outside. A Samsonite that he could have sworn rested under his feet in a bus would metamorphose outside the window as the prize being fought over, apparently to death, by two urchins seeking the honour of carrying it. And it was all done through osmosis. He never actually saw his bags move, never actually lost a piece, but he never found one where he had left it either.

At the airport car park he hastily turned around, ready

to go back to look and found a small taxi driver anxiously dogging him, lugging the suitcase and inconceivably still nurturing hopes of Chris patronage. An irate yell from Ajai caused him to abandon the suitcase and scurry off, casting looks of bereavement at Chris.

They arrived at a car and were greeted by a man Chris took to be Ajay's friend.

"Hi," said Chris warmly, thrusting out his hand at the man who gaped at him before reaching inside the car and putting on a chauffeur's cap.

Sheepishly Chris settled back as they drove away. 'I must remember to get my TB shots tomorrow', he suddenly recalled, worried again.

He looked curiously out of the window, but it was dark outside. 'It could be anywhere,' he thought. The excitement, the concern, the numbness began to ebb and he started to drowse. He barely recalled arriving, stumbling into the room set aside for him and falling into an exhausted sleep.

The next month had sped by in a blur. Not only did he have to adjust to India, but he had to try and understand the complexities of the labour problems besetting KapCo. 'Its hard to concentrate on personnel demands when you are trying to adjust to a cow contentedly chewing the cud in the middle of an intensely crowded street.' He had found nobody else paying the slightest attention to the animal and began to feel that perhaps he was a little peculiar in noticing the sight. He was surprised at how soon he had got used to it.

Now after a month, lazing in his room, he tried to figure out his feelings about India. Overall, he thought, it fascinated him. It was as though the entire city was a vast replica of what America must have been like in the days of the Gold

Rush. There were crowds everywhere, the streets seemed like gladiatorial combats with warriors riding on every conceivable kind of steed. He couldn't believe the diversity of traffic. Push carts, buses, Mercedes Benz, horse drawn carriages, trucks emitting villainous fumes, strange three wheeled contraptions like over fed rodents, all sorts of Indian cars dashing into apparently impenetrable traffic and emerging untouched, buses from which human forms emerged out of every orifice like strange new toadstools, diverse two wheelers driven as though each rider was armour plated and therefore heedless of potential collision. And of course people everywhere.

He had expected much of this of course, but he had adjusted to it because of the strange feeling that everybody he met or passed on the street had made a little space for him. In America, he remembered a Lebanese friend telling him, he had always felt that there was a field of ice around Americans, for all their friendliness, beyond which he could not penetrate. Here, Chris felt that the sunshine had perhaps melted that ice. Of course he was chased by beggars and beckoned by shopkeepers, but he felt strangely accepted.

What he had not accepted was the chaotic sprawl of shops and hawkers and other roadside entrepreneurs who made walking the equivalent of a steeplechase. Chris had initially wondered if the shops had come up first, with streets being squeezed in afterwards, wherever there was space. Of course when he had gone down the same streets late at night, he had realised that the city was actually quite well laid out, but there were too many people competing for the same space.

The dust and the fumes had annoyed him the most. But seeing the commercial frenzy on the sidewalks, he had decided that the priorities were first to do business and later to look into the problems caused by pollution.

'They'll have to look into it some time or the other,' he had thought resignedly. And that had been another odd feature, he mused, how the vastness of the human mass caused him to become resigned about a situation that would have roused considerable indignation if he had seen it in America.

Of course it was easier to be dismissive about it when he was living in an area like Punjabi Bagh with houses every bit as smart as anything in America, and with lawns around them. The Kapoor house was circled by a high wall with several rooms near the entrance which were the domain of Mr. Sunder. Chris had the bedroom at the extreme edge of the main house which comprised six bedrooms and three sitting rooms. Various servants flitted about and adjusting to them had really been a problem.

It was only lately that he had stopped thanking them whenever one had brought something for him. They had gawked at his friendliness initially but he still couldn't accept their silent presence everywhere. They seemed like zombies who didn't expect to be noticed, or thanked and who felt it was quite normal for them to waft into his room, tidy his cupboard, take away dirty linen, sweep the room, or deposit his meal tray if he wanted to eat alone. Chris had begun to suspect that they were actually robots who lay lifeless in Mr. Sunder's kingdom until one was activated to wheel about doing errands.

But overall Chris felt at home. He was in a modern city with high rises and yet with broad tree-lined streets with vast mansions and in clusters everywhere, those pockets of frantic shopping. Of course the fact that Ajay Vir was always around had helped him settle down and he couldn't deny the benefits of having a well-ordered home to return to at the end of the day.

He thought of Ajai Vir and how similar he was to other American young men of his age. In fact how both of them were in nearly identical situations with successful fathers having established businesses that they would one day inherit. 'Of course,' Chris thought with a grin, 'Ajay Vir's father is a little more, what's the word, 'colourful' than my own, but he had really come up the hard way.'

Ajay Vir had told him of how the old man, Ram Avtar, had arrived in Delhi after the partition of India with nothing except the clothes he wore. His parents had been killed during the riots in what later became Pakistan and Ram Avtar was left with a young wife to look after. He had started with a hand cart from which he sold utensils that he got on credit, pushing the cart from door to door. From that beginning he had built up the business to a point where it now had a turnover of some US $ 30 million a year.

"Anyway," Ajai Vir had told him on the first day, "I'm telling you all this because the old man's quite a character. So don't get put off or anything by him, because he's actually very well meaning and one smart cookie despite his eccentricities."

"Sure, sure," Chris had reassured him, while wondering what the oddities could be, "no problem."

"In that case," Ajai Vir had sighed, rising, "I may as well show you the rest of the house and get it over with."

Puzzled, Chris had followed and after ten minutes returned with a face he could barely keep straight.

"You see what I mean," Ajai Vir had practically blushed.

"No, no," Chris reassured him, "I think its great. Really neat."

Ajai Vir had grinned at him and left.

Each room had been fitted with a bar, including the bathrooms and boasted of a small, plastic chandelier with lights in three different colours. Depending on which rack you lifted a bottle from, the chandelier would emit the appropriate light. Green for beer, blue for gin and red for whisky. Simultaneously, a recorder somewhere would play 'Jingle Bells'. This did not change with the drink.

They had also gone to Ajai Vir's room who had pushed opened the door with a deep breath. The first thing Chris saw as he entered was a tall blackboard with B.B.B written on it in chalk.

"Every morning, I have to erase it and write it again so that I remember it for the rest of the day".

"What does it mean?" asked the perplexed Chris.

"Its my father's theory of the three secrets of doing business."

"Which is?"

"Butter them. Bribe them. Or Bash them".

"Perfect", applauded Chris, "The Harvard Business School couldn't teach you better. When do I meet your Dad?"

"Oh he'll be back soon. He leaves home early for the factory".

The factory had been beset by a very severe labour problem, Chris had gathered, because of the emergence of a young labour leader to whom the factory union had switched allegiance. The earlier union head was an old KapCo employee who had kept the union docile so long as he had personally been kept content with bribes of various sorts. But the workers had recently voted him out and invited the rising star of the

11

area, named Prabal Kumar, to head their union. This guy, Chris gathered, was young, charismatic, prone to violence and keen to establish his reputation.

The factory had been rocked by agitations since his arrival. Numerous meetings had been held, but every time the KapCo management agreed to one set of demands, Prabal Kumar had raised a fresh one. It had begun to appear to the management that Kumar was more intent on causing a strike with the resultant publicity than getting a better deal for the workers. However, there was no way to persuade the workers about this. They saw Prabal as the man who would get them more than they had dared ask.

Ram Avtar Kapoor had gone to the concerned ministry in the Central Government in the hope that they might intervene and prevent the strike that seemed to be developing. He sought and received an appointment with the Minister, Sevak Chand.

The Minister greeted him warmly as Kapoor walked in. Of course they had met socially earlier, but they had not met on official business. Sevak Chand was extremely tall, nearly seven feet, and legendary for his courtesy, his thread bare clothes, and his devotion to attributing everything he said to either Mahatma Gandhi or Pundit Nehru or some other Indian Prime Minister. He was in his late 60's, lean as a bamboo and his voice rarely rose above a guttural whisper. With him was his Personal Assistant, known to the world only as Sharmaji.

Kapoor had sat down, made his speech and waited for the Minister to speak.

"Yes," said the Minister softly, "I am knowing about Prabal Kumar. He says he is working for the people day and night and many of my own people have met him."

Kapoor brightened at this sign of a potential tiff between the Minister and Prabal.

"But", resumed the Minister accurately reading Kapoor's response, "he has not swayed any of my workers." He fell silent.

"Sir", enquired Kapoor, puzzled, "what shall I do?"

"As Nehruji said, 'play the game in the spirit of the game,'" the Minister replied, pressing a bell to signal that the audience was over.

2

As the first workers of the morning shift trudged towards the open factory gates, a taxi drew up beside them. Four men jumped out.

"You can't go in," said one of them, barring the way of the workers.

The workers recognised the four as office bearers of the factory union.

"Why?" one asked the person blocking his way, though he suspected he knew already. In answer, the union official simply jerked his thumb backwards at the other three men who had come with him.

Two had scaled one of the pillars on either side of the huge wrought iron gates and were sitting on top of it. One held a short stick with a small rectangular red flag on it and the other passed a rope around it and all around the pillar so that it was held upright tightly. Then he tied it into a knot with two quick hitches that displayed much practise. Taking a knife from his pocket, he flicked it open, cut the rope and both men jumped down to go across to the other pillar to put up a similar flag.

The fourth man was standing in front of the pillar to the left of the gate. He had several rolls of paper in one hand and a can with glue and brush in the other. He unrolled one sheet, smeared the glue on the back of the paper and slapped it on the pillar. Carefully he smoothened it with his hand so that it was stuck flat.

The small group of workers near the union official could read it from fifteen feet away.

'Strike'

The red letter stood out boldly. Below it was written in smaller size 'KāpCo Industries workers on strike. Meet our just demands.' By then the second roll of paper had also been pasted next to the strike poster. This said, 'Our Demands.' It listed thirty two, ranging from higher salaries to increased overtime allowance and ended with 'Taxi fare for all workers from nearest bus stop to factory gate.' This last point had aroused considerable debate among the union officials since the bus stop at which most workers alighted was about fifty feet from the factory gate. However, it was finally included as one of the bargaining chips to be given away to the management during the hectic negotiations that would doubtlessly follow.

The number of workers had rapidly swelled as more people arrived to report for work. They saw the flags fluttering, the notices pasted, and milled about restlessly. They grinned at each other in excitement mixed with uncertainty and some anxiety. Certainly it had been building up to this for a month, ever since Prabal Kumar arrived at this same gate and delivered a speech that suddenly showed them how much more they could get for their labours. But still, it was one thing to talk, even to demonstrate and raise slogans, another to actually strike. And hadn't the *maalik* been good to them? Hadn't he after all been like one of them, starting his career as a ʾnan who rode his bicycle through Delhi, selling the utensils piled behind him?

True, if this fellow Prabal could get them even half of what he had promised, they would be getting three times their current wages, but supposing it didn't work? And then what were they supposed to live on while the strike was on? So when the union official barring their way sensed their uneasiness and raised the cry of "Long live Prabal Kumar", their response was feeble.

Quickly he changed the slogan.

"We demand our rights", he shouted. "What do we demand?" he asked.

This time their shout was more full throated. "Our rights", they said.

"What do we demand?" he shouted again.

"Our rights". This time it was a roar.

"Our rights," he chanted and they picked up the refrain, "Our rights, our rights, our rights, our rights." The roar continued and grew in volume as more workers arrived.

The guards at the factory gates who had been waiting to see if any of the workers would break ranks and enter the factory, began to push the heavy gates shut. The workers saw the gates begin to close inexorably and began to chant even louder. The loudness of their voices, the sense of solidarity, even the hypnotic rhythm of their chant gave them a feeling of confidence.

Yet when the gates shut with a clang, every one of them flinched, and in their hearts there was fear because all of them knew of strikes that had failed, where workers had lost terribly, yet they also knew of many cases when they had won greatly. So they chanted even louder, because now with the closing of the gates the battle had begun. How long it would go on, what sacrifices would have to be made, they didn't know, but they did know that they were prepared to fight for as long as it took to get as many of their demands as they could.

The head of KapCo's security, Capt. A.S. Singh, who

had joined the company after retiring from the army, looked at the chanting mob through the grilled window of his office adjacent to the gates. He held a telephone receiver in his hand and spoke to the Manager of the factory, Lal Verma, who was in his office, having reached that morning half an hour before the first worker.

"Sir," said Singh, "its begun. No one broke ranks and I have shut the gates before they decided to come in and cause violence."

"Has there been any violence yet?" asked Verma.

"Not yet sir. They're simply raising slogans."

"Is Prabal Kumar there?" asked Verma.

"No sir, only his assistants. He may come later in the day when the men of the second shift also arrive."

'He may indeed,' thought Verma sardonically. 'He certainly enjoys a larger audience than a single shift crowd.'

He picked up a dial-less telephone on his desk, an instrument plugged into the hotline that connected the factory at Faridabad to Delhi. "Get me Kapoor sahib," he told the factory operator.

For once the hotline was working and Verma was soon talking to Mr. Sunder.

"Sethiji is doing his prayers", said Mr. Sunder. "Is it important enough to disturb him?" Mr. Sunder controlled access to Mr. Kapoor at his house and he wasn't about to let any of the executives forget it, even if they outranked him.

"It is", said Verma curtly.

"Perhaps I can pass on the message," suggested Sunder, who really didn't like Verma very much. "You know I am the first person he sees every morning."

"Good," said Verma. "Kindly tell him the workers have gone on strike and we have shut the factory gates."

"I'll get him on the phone right away," said Mr. Sunder who had long ago learned it was wiser not to be the carrier of bad news.

The phone trilled on the table just outside the little prayer room Ram Avtar Kapoor had built in an alcove inside his bedroom. The little cubicle was dark and nearly bare in contrast to the opulence of the rest of the bedroom.

On a small table covered by a white cloth were three pictures, one of Lakshmi, the goddess of prosperity, one of Shiva the destroyer and curiously, a little to one side, a black and white picture of Kapoor's wife who had died eighteen years ago.

The photograph had been taken when she had only had a few weeks to live after a battle with cancer that had lasted for a long year. The suffering and pain had marked her face and there were lines that looked like they had been drawn with a pen, particularly since her skin looked so pale and fragile as to be translucent. It was a face of great gentleness, of someone who had seen much agony but borne it with courage. The eyes had a warmth and kindness to them that came through even in the photograph.

Kapoor had nearly worshipped her when she was alive and he actually did so now that she was dead. As usual, every morning, he was thinking of her, just as he had every day on waking for the last eighteen years since she had died. He sometimes wondered if the pictures of the other deities weren't just an excuse to enable him to pray in front of her photograph.

He couldn't remember a time when he hadn't known her. Their families were neighbours in one of the little alleys of Lahore and when she was born and he was a mere five years old, their parents had decided that the children should

18

be married later. When he was seventeen and she twelve, they had been wedded. Immediately thereafter he had gone away to study at a college, but before that there had been years of watching, growing, of playing with her, "I can remember you wetting me when I first picked you up," he used to tease her in later years, "how many husbands can claim that?"

The burring phone interrupted his thoughts. He let it ring for a while, half sensing what the call was about. He let himself indulge in the weakness of missing his wife for another few seconds, a weakness that strangely enough strengthened him for the challenges of the day. Then he picked up the phone and listened to Lal Verma at the other end.

"I see," is all Kapoor said. So its begun, he thought to himself. The first ever strike in the 35 years since he had set up the factory. It was a problem he would have to resolve by himself. Ajai Vir was too young, too idealistic to handle the rough times ahead, but he could learn from this too. He wished he were closer to his son who had been educated at the best boarding schools and colleges, but had grown up away from home. Besides which, in one unwise moment when he had been particularly annoyed with Ajay Vir over some trivial disagreement, he had told his son. "The first priority in my life is the company. You are my only child, but you come second."

Since then Ajay Vir had devoted nearly all his time to the company, but there had been an unbridgeable chasm between them. 'It doesn't matter,' thought Kapoor, 'so long as he learns enough to keep the company moving when I'm gone. That will be my way of being remembered.' But first he had to make sure that KapCo survived this crisis.

Kapoor carefully combed the last remaining strands

of hair on his head and went out, a medium sized figure tending to plumpness, bespectacled, in a brown safari suit. He walked down the corridor to Ajay Vir's room, knocked and walked in. His son was ready to leave and looked surprised as Kapoor sat down.

"Its started," said Kapoor. "They've gone on strike. Tell me, which of the three B's should we use?"

"Its probably wise to bribe Prabal Kumar as well as the workers," suggested Ajai Vir. "Its too late to butter them and we don't have the kind of mind required to try and bash anyone."

Kapoor nodded. The boy's logic is sensible, he thought, but good sense never broke a strike.

Father and son walked out to the car that would take them to the factory and acknowledged the chauffeur's salute. They sat back as he started the car and drove away.

Chris woke up an hour later as the smell of hot tea filled his room. The servant who had brought the tea tray slipped away. Chris sat down by the window, sipping his tea, a habit he had picked up in India. He beheld Mr. Sunder coming towards him and braced himself.

"They have gone on strike," informed Mr. Sunder. "I do not know what is to become of this country when it is full of such wretched people. I think there are no strikes in America," he announced. "That is how the country has become so great. But India will go to dogs with such scoundrels I am telling to you."

An old woman dressed in a sari silently entered and began to dust the room. She was, Chris had learned, a lady called Tai by everybody, which means Father's elder sister. She had no discernible role as far as Chris could see, but was kept on since she had been with the family for years and had practically brought up Ajai Vir during his mother's long illness and thereafter whenever he came home on vacations.

Chris had found the presence of servants pervasive and irritating but he had learned how much easier life became with them around.

Mr. Sunder was still hovering nearby, clearly ill at ease.

"I am reading lots about America," he said finally, fidgeting. "But I am not finding any reliable magazine. Are you having any?"

"Well, nothing immediately," said Chris, "but I can get some. Which one do you want?"

"Anything good," said Mr. Sunder. "Something about social affairs to give me really true picture."

"Well, maybe I could get you Cosmopolitan. They do a lot on social affairs."

"No, not that way. I am meaning some really social magazine that will me give true picture." He shuffled his feet and looked penetratingly out of the window.

"Such as?" enquired Chris.

"Oh," said Mr. Sunder very casually, "I am hearing lot many things about social magazine like Playboy and Penthouse. Of course I am never seeing before," be began to mumble, his spectacles shining. "But if you are having I will take to my friends who are wanting to know. Of course I am not interested, but for sake of my friends I am asking."

"Naturally, of course" soothed Chris. "I am sure your friends will be interested. I don't have any right now, but I'll see what I can do."

"Of course you are not mentioning this to Ajai Vir, I hope. He may be not understanding."

"Naturally not," agreed Chris.

"I hope," said Mr. Sunder anxiously, "you are not thinking all Indians are wanting to see all such magazines. I am only asking for sake of some friends. You are not thinking I hope that all Indians are like this."

"No, of course", reassured Chris. "In fact I don't even think of Indians as being different from me. I just think of Indians as being Americans whose freckles have joined."

Much relieved, but puzzled at what freckles might be, Mr. Sunder departed.

Chris grinned to himself. Social magazines, he thought with a chuckle. At least the guy is normal. He took a shower and dressed, waiting for Kalpana to arrive.

Kalpana Singh was Ajai Vir's girlfriend and they were planning to get married as soon as the labour problems got resolved. She was the daughter of a minor royal family that had fallen on hard times. But the old aura of royalty still interested people and opened doors. Ram Avtar Kapoor approved of the match simply because, as he informed Ajai Vir, Kalpana's family had excellent contacts among other royal descendants, many of whom were doing exceedingly well in politics.

Kalpana lived by herself in a small apartment nearby, since her parents preferred to live in their crumbling palace somewhere in the foothills of the Himalayas. She was 24 years old, tall, dusky, worked with a garment exporter, and Chris thought she was one of the most beautiful girls he had ever seen in his life. He was also in a dilemma, because he sensed that she reciprocated his interest. However, there was the small matter of Ajai Vir and the possible repercussions on their business arrangement if matters got out of hand. Also, he didn't know what the other ramifications would be if news of an affair leaked out. Would he have to marry her?

Would Ajai Vir shoot them both? He was planning to raise the subject in an indirect way this time when she came to take him on yet another sightseeing trip around Delhi. These excursions had the full blessings of Ajai Vir who saw it as a good way to keep Chris entertained, which duty he would have had to perform otherwise.

Chris saw the gates open and Kalpana's red Maruti appeared. He went out and they drove away.

"Where to this time?" he enquired.

"We're going to see the Qutub Minar. Its a tower that was built for some reason or the other and its really very interesting".

Chris braced himself for the wild chariot race that was the normal Delhi traffic and throughout the ride kept pressing imaginary brakes. Kalpana noticed it again and laughed at him.

"You're an over-protected Yank," she giggled. "You'll have to learn to think in terms of missing the other car by millimeters rather than yards like you do. Its quite safe. I've never had an accident."

Chris ungritted his teeth and tried to calm down. He became more aware of her proximity and the perfume she was wearing. Kalpana's hand brushed his leg everytime she changed gears. 'This', Chris thought, 'is unbearable. How exactly should I broach the subject?'

When the Qutab Minar, a minaret several hundred feet in height came into view, he was struck by inspiration.

"Doesn't it look," he asked, "like some guy with the world's most severe case of hard on?"

Kalpana laughed, "I've seen better." She looked him in the eye.

They were walking towards the base of the tower. "How's

that?" asked Chris. "I always thought Indian girls were virgins till they got married."

"That was in another century. Today almost no one is. And one or two experiences don't really count."

"You mean they have their fun, get married and become good, faithful wives."

"Good yes, faithful no."

"What does that mean?"

"It means the fun really starts after they get married."

"You're joking?"

"Not really."

"You mean I have a chance with Indian girls."

"Of course. More than Indian men."

"Why?"

"Because you're safe. You won't tell your friends about it and a girl won't lose her reputation. Besides you'll return home and there won't be any complications later."

"I'm shocked,"

"Don't be. Its all quite civilised."

"What if the husband finds out?"

"Usually they never do. And even if they do, so what? They're usually having affairs on the side too."

"Amazing. But it must be among the elite only."

"Well yes, but also among the poorest people. And even the middle class is catching up. The only rule is "Don't get caught and don't cause a scandal."

"I think you better stop. You're giving me ideas."

"I certainly don't intend to." She gave him a half smile.

They reached the base of the tower but Chris wasn't really paying attention. They dutifully circumnavigated it and then went to see a nearby iron pillar that was a metallurgical marvel since it hadn't rusted for centuries despite being exposed to the elements. Chris couldn't concentrate on that either. Kalpana brushed against him and giggled again.

"You're starting to look like the iron pillar yourself," she said innocently. "Whatever could be the matter?"

"Nothing, nothing, I was just thinking that you really live in an ancient castle."

"I see. Old castles excite you, do they?"

"Absolutely," said Chris, regaining control of himself, "do you have pictures of the place?'

"Probably, but they're locked up somewhere. You're sure you want to see them?" she teased.

"However distasteful the job, duty is duty as Hitler used to say."

They walked back to the car and went to her apartment.

"Would you like some water?" She asked as she opened the door.

Chris reached out for her as they stepped inside and she came into his arms. "I would like you," he said as they embraced.

Later, when they both lay back naked and exhausted, he noticed with surprise that they hadn't even made it till the bedroom. He was also surprised by her skill.

"You and Ajai Vir must be practising this quite a bit." He checked to see if she was displeased.

"Sort of," she stretched languorously. "Though I have a strict rule for him."

"Which is?"

"Only above the waist and below the knees."

Chris laughed. "Why?" he blew on a strand of wet hair across her cheek.

"Oh, good Indian girl and all that you know. Saving myself

25

for my wedding night. And not a word about this from you."
She grabbed a chunk of his hair.

"Ow, ow, okay. Scout's honour."

She let go and got up stretching.

'She's gorgeous' thought Chris, desire stirring again.

"Not now," she said, slapping away his outstretched hand.
"Time to get back."

'Yes, Memsahib', thought Chris. 'I've done my duty!'
he thought with surprise. 'Its as though I've been used. She
wasn't involved emotionally. I was just a useful, well, tool?'
He grinned sardonically to himself. 'But who am I to complain?' he thought complacently, remembering the last half
hour.

She drove him back to the house.

"I hope I'll see you soon?" asked Chris.

"May be," she said casually. She drove off.

Matters hadn't been going as well for Ajai Vir and his
father. The workers were gathered outside the factory and
as soon as they saw the car they began raising slogans. But
they parted to let the car through, which drove to the factory.

Now they were seated in Ram Avtar's room with Lal
Verma.

"The Central Government is not going to help", said
Ram Avtar, "I've been to see Sevak Chand."

"What do we do now?" asked Verma.

"I think only the Government can pressure the workers.
We have to find a way to make them act."

"How?" asked Ajai Vir.

"Two things", said Ram Avtar. "First, we must instigate
violence so that there is wide publicity. Second, we should
plant stories in the press about what a good man Prabal Kumar
is and how much he is trying to do for the workers."

Ajay Vir looked incredulous. "Dad, Dad," he broke in, "I would have thought we should do the opposite. We should get the press to attack him so that he'll back off."

"No," cautioned his father. "Any attack in the press will make him seem like a martyr. He'll claim its a capitalist controlled press. But if they praise him, it might force Sevak Chand to act because Delhi is his power base and Prabal could be a threat to him if he becomes too popular. We have to try and make Sevak see it that way.

Ajay Vir tried to digest this. "And the violence?" he asked cautiously.

"Oh that's easy enough. Verma, you know where men are available. You make sure that a few mingle with the workers and when one of the senior managers is going in or out, he is attacked and then they stone the factory and light a few fires. Bonfires always look good in the papers. And Verma, make sure that some of our friends in the press are present to take pictures." He paused and bent forward. "Verma, this could be the most important assignment of your life. If you handle it well, I'll put you on the board of directors of the company and I promise you that money will never be a problem for you ever again." But Ram's Avtar's eyes narrowed and Ajai Vir couldn't remember him looking so dangerous before, "not a word to anyone else. Is that clear?"

"Yes sir," Verma bobbed his head. "You can depend on me sir."

He got up, as Ram Avtar motioned him away. "But keep me informed at every step, all right?"

"Yes sir," bowed Verma as he let himself out of the room.

"Can he be trusted?" asked Ajai Vir, still stunned by his father's cunning.

"Yes. He has money problems and he knows he'll be well paid for this."

"What else do we do now?"

"We cultivate the local policemen. They can be crucial. And you start taking your journalist friends out to dinner and wine and dine them as well as you can. Spare no expense."

"Sure, Dad," Ajai Vir felt inadequate in the situation. "Anything you say."

Later that evening over dinner, Ajai Vir recounted the plan to Chris. Tai silently brought the dishes to the table where the chair at the head was empty since Ram Avtar had stayed behind at the factory.

Chris was suitable impressed at the scheme. "I guess we still have a lot to learn from our fathers. Mine is a shrewd old character too. That's why they've made it, I guess. I mean we're both pretty smart too, but most of what we know is theoretical stuff."

"Yeah, I suppose so," agreed Ajai Vir, "but its still frustrating for me. I mean I've learned so much from business school back in the States, but here all that seems to count is who you know and how much you've paid him. Besides, I'd like to do bigger things. I mean the business has a turnover of about 30 million dollars and we could be at least four times that if Dad would allow us to make a public issue and invite capital. We're still a Private Limited Company and our own resources aren't going to let us expand at the speed we should. I mean its really frustrating to read Fortune magazine and hear about how the rest of the world is expanding into billion dollar corporations, while we're stuck with these dumb kitchen utensils."

"I know how you feel," agreed Chris "We're supposed

to be public limited, but the entire shareholding is with the family. It's great too because we don't have to worry about takeover bids, but we're not exactly a threat to IBM with the plastic buckets we make. Anyway," he concluded, "there's nothing we can do I guess until our Dads retire."

"You mean," grinned Ajai Vir, "until they kick the bucket."

Both roared with laughter. "Yeah," chuckled Chris, "whether plastic or stainless steel. By the way," he added, "I've been in India for a month and I still haven't seen the Taj Mahal. That's probably a crime of some sort ... Am I needed in Delhi or can I make a trip to Agra?"

"Sure, go ahead. I'll get Sunder to fix the tickets."

"Fix" is probably the right word, thought Chris. Any place else in the world, it would be 'get' the tickets. But in India, he'd found, the simplest things were the most complex. The act of getting a ticket to India's most visited spot would inevitably require all sorts of incredible manoeuvring. In fact, he suspected that the more popular a destination, the more difficult it would be to get there. It was as if Agra was situated in the middle of a forest with an undergrowth of red tape all around it for hundreds of miles, like red barbed wire requiring immense courage, perseverance and skill to traverse. However, the Sunders of India seemed born with the skill of finding a reasonably comfortable track through the jungle.

3

Two days later, Chris was at the New Delhi Railway Station at 5.30 in the morning, looking for the Shatabdi Express that would take him to Agra. He was possessively clutching assorted bits of paper that would get him there. He thought yet again of the Indian passion for paper. 'India will be the very last country in the world to change to a paperless way of life,' he thought. Perhaps the paper held a particularly exalted place in the culture because so much of the population was illiterate or recently literate and a paper denoted education and mysterious, omnipotent authority. Unless something was on paper, it seemed to lack reality.

Now he looked around the station at the bodies sprawled everywhere and marvelled at the Indian ability to create a home with invisible walls of privacy in the most public environment conceivable. People slept as soundly as if they were in their own bedrooms. A certain spot was the toilet judging from the smells emanating and this was tacitly agreed to by everyone, though why they chose one spot and not another was unclear. Having established their territory, a family would place its luggage to mark the boundaries as well as to prevent theft and drift off immediately to deep sleep as though the clamour, the smells, the surging mass, the brilliant lights, didn't exist at all. A few people could be seen asleep without any luggage and Chris wondered if they had become so accustomed to railway stations that though they actually lived in Delhi, they chose to spend their nights snoozing on platforms.

Shaking himself out of this reverie, Chris strode briskly

to the gate and let the official rummage among the papers Chris had till he found one that pleased him. Finding the train was easy enough and Chris boarded it.

The carriage was lined with chairs and Chris found one that had the same number as his ticket. It was adjacent to the window and Chris sank into it. In a while, just as the train started off, a man appeared and put his suitcase into the overhead rack. He then seated himself beside Chris and subjected him to a close scrutiny.

"What is your good name?" he asked.

"I'm Chris." They shook hands.

"Where you are from?"

"Ah, the United States."

"You are having own house there?"

"Sorry?"

"You are owning own home in USA?"

"Well no," conceded Chris, suppressing the impulse to tell him to mind his own damn business. "Actually we're still paying off the mortgage."

"Ah," beamed the man, "I am owning own home in Delhi." Pleased by this sign of his superiority, he introduced himself. "Myself is Subramanium, I am working in Accounts Department of Government."

They shook hands. "You are married?" he next asked Chris.

"No," confessed Chris.

"Very bad. Everyone should marry and settle down. I am married, why you are not?."

"Well, I haven't found the right person I guess."

"Not good. Not good at all. In our ancient books it is written all things must be done in right time. You are reading *Mahabharata*?"

"Well, I am planning to," said Chris a little desperately.

"You may kindly do so at earliest. It is part of our glorious culture. You are wanting to break your fast?"

"What? Oh, I see, breakfast. No thanks, I ate before I came."

"Good. Then I think I will tell you about *Mahabharata*."

"Actually, I'm quite hungry. I think I will have breakfast. Where do I get it from?"

"Not to worry. Waiter. Waiter is bringing some. Also, there is tea. But you are wanting soft or hard."

Chris flexed his muscles. The train had gathered speed and he wondered if he could throw himself out of the door, or better still fling Mr. Subramanium out. Then realisation dawned that this wasn't a sexual pass. "Oh you mean do I want a soft drink or hard liquor. I'll take something soft please."

"I am non-drinker also. It is very bad habit. You are vegetarian or non-veg?"

"I'm non-veg."

"What your father does?"

"He makes plastic buckets."

"Why?"

"What do you mean why? Its his business."

"Oh you are having own business. That is good. How many brothers and sisters you are having?"

"None actually. I'm the only child."

"Very bad. Everyone must have two children. Why your parents are not?"

"I'll write and ask," promised Chris.

Breakfast was served in trays and Chris gingerly tried the omelette. It was surprisingly good. He gobbled up the rest, closing his ears to Mr. Subramanium's squishy breakfast serenade.

Chris looked out of the window. "Good grief," he said in disgust and alarm. An entire army of defecating bottoms looked him in the eye. Men, women, children, a horde seemed to have trekked to the railway line to perform their morning ablutions with the express intent of revolting him.

"Ah yes," said Mr. Subramanium. "They are doing morning job."

"They do this in public view every day."

"They are poor people. They are not having anywhere else to go. You may draw curtains if you are so wishing."

Chris did so and to prevent further inquisition, or a commentary on the subtleties of the *Mahabharata*, pretended to fall asleep.

When he next opened his eyes, he found he had actually dozed off and the train was approaching Agra. Mr. Subramanium had disappeared so Chris got off by himself. He walked out and got into the first taxi he saw.

"The Taj Mahal," he said.

The taxi took him through a dusty, crowded, ancient town that couldn't have changed much from the Mughal days except for the din of car horns, auto rickshaw smoke and tinkling of bicycle bells. Its not much of an introduction to what is said to be the world's most beautiful building, he thought, already a bit disappointed.

So when he actually saw the Taj, he was stunned by its splendour. "Jeez," he breathed. "This is serious shit." He spent the day prowling around it, memorising its lattice work, its ornamentation, its sheer beauty. He was humbled as never before in his life. And all for the love of a woman, he thought on the train ride back to Delhi. Its a bit of cold sperm solidified into marble and frozen for all time, a reminder of the Emperor Shah Jahan as much as of his wife, Mumtaz Mahal.

33

With such genius among the Indians, he thought as the taxi drove him out of the chaos of New Delhi railway station, why didn't they apply just a bit of it to creating slightly less congested cities?

A few days later he was informed that Sharmaji, the Personal Assistant to Sevak Chand, was coming to the Kapoors for a private dinner. "You might find it interesting if you want to join us," Ajai Vir told Chris.

Chris decided to skip lunch that day, having learned the hard way that dinners organised by the Indian rich were long and awesomely sumptuous. The first time he went to one, he gorged everything in sight until midnight, then learned to his horror that what he had eaten were only the snacks, what were called 'light refreshments'. The real food started only thereafter.

Everytime Chris went to one of these dinners anywhere in Delhi, he wondered how anyone could believe that India was full of starving people. He had never before seen so many people eat so much from such a wide selection. It was common for Chinese, Indian and Continental cuisines to be on offer at the same dinner. In fact Chris couldn't really characterise them as mere dinners anymore, preferring to think of them as events. Something in the nature of culinary Olympics.

Part of it, he surmised, had to do with one-up-manship. What had been served by one host had to be matched if not surpassed by his social peers. And some of the showmanship was probably a consequence of the poverty that undeniably did exist. It was a means of celebrating that you were not one of the poor. Besides which, Indians plainly and simply liked to eat a lot. Chris had only started to discover that the curry he had all along equated with Indian food was only a small part of the vast culinary treasure grove that was India.

However Sharmaji's dinner was to be a private affair, without the hordes that usually accompanied Indian parties. So Chris was prepared for a more measured pace. Whatever was to be discussed was to be private. "We're going to try the 'B' for Bribery tonight, aren't we?" he shrewdly asked Ajai Vir, who only grinned.

Though the time was set for 8.00 PM, when Chris walked into the main living room he saw Ajai Vir wandering around with shaving cream on his face.

"Ran out of blades," he explained.

"Aren't you late?" asked Chris.

"Nah. He'll never get here before 9.00."

Left to his own devices, Chris ambled away to hold discussions with Mr. Sunder. But even he was busy.

"Very VIP dinner tonight," he informed Chris. "I don't know how I will manage," he protested, shuffling papers importantly, though what his papers had to do with dinner Chris couldn't imagine. He didn't even have time to enquire about the socially meaningful magazines Chris had promised to get. Chris went back to his room till the sound of a car told him Sharmaji had arrived. Apparently even Kalpana hadn't been invited so as not to inhibit Sharmaji in case the Kapoors were successful in getting him to let his hair down.

Chris waited till he heard the music of Jingle Bells repeated at a gratifying speed which indicated that all was going well. Then he strolled in and was introduced as 'our foreign collaborator.'

Sharmaji had oily dark skin that shone like his hair. He had a large paunch that stuck out and was visible in the gaps between the buttons of his grey safari suit. He had a drink in his hand which he splashed about to welcome Chris.

Ram Avtar took it as a sign to refill Sharmaji's glass and Jingle Bells was heard again.

"What your company is doing in U.S.?" asked Sharmaji.

"We're in the plastics business."

"Ah," Sharmaji's eyes narrowed, "so KapCo is expanding from steel utensils."

"Only with your blessings," cringed Ram Avtar.

"That is of course always there."

"Yes, Sharma sahib, we are very happy to know that, but there are always some problems with which we are having to bother you."

"Later, later," boomed Sharmaji, "it is too early to discuss business."

Ram Avtar laughed at Sharmaji's wit and changed the subject, always making sure that Sharmaji had the last word.

Whenever he felt Sharmaji had ventured what could be construed to be a joke, he roared with laughter. He had a truly formidable laugh. It emerged from the depths of his belly and issued forth in whatever tone seemed appropriate. Sometimes it was ribald, at others deferential. Sometimes convulsive, at others fraternal. It was believed in business circles that Ram Avtar had secured large contracts purely on the strength of his laugh. Chris could well believe it.

Watching Ram Avtar and Sharmaji, he felt as though he was watching a bullfight, with Sharmaji as the toreador and Ram Avtar as the bull. No matter how much Ram Avtar laughed and how often he refilled Sharmaji's glass, Sharmaji's eyes stayed slits of black. He knew exactly what Ram Avtar was up to and he knew precisely what he wanted from him as well. So he teased Ram Avtar, drawing him near, letting him get within breathing distance, then like a master bull fighter teasingly letting him graze past. At other times he edged tantalising close, then mockingly stepped aside as though with a flourish.

Despite the cool evening, Ram Avtar's face was flushed and sweaty. He knew how desperately he needed Sharmaji's help and so did Sharmaji. Dinner was served and they sat down to eat a succession of dishes. At the end of it, Sharmaji burped in contentment, having demolished three different kinds of Indian desserts.

"Now Kapoor sahib," he stretched his feet out, "what service I can do for you? I am only a small man."

"No no, how you can say that," protested Ram Avtar, wondering if Sharmaji was still teasing, "you are the one who runs the Government of India."

"Not at all," boomed Sharmaji, quite pleased by this outrageous lie, "but perhaps, I have earned some respect."

"The world knows you are the main force in the Ministry. Not a mouse moves without your consent."

"Hee hee hee," chortled Sharmaji, "not at all, not at all," practically begging Ram Avtar to carry on.

"Politicians are all very well," ventured Ram Avtar daringly, "but the world knows who is really who." He stopped in case he had gone too far.

"They are saying this about me in business circles?" asked Sharmaji.

"Everybody well knows it."

"I see, *achaa*, I see. Then surely I must fulfill my reputation. Now what is your problem?"

"We need the Government to help us break this strike."

"That is a big thing you are asking," said Sharmaji, "a very big thing."

"That is why I have come to a big man," flattered Ram Avtar, "otherwise I would have gone to a small man."

"That is also true," conceded Sharmaji.

"And whatever the expenses involved," hinted Ram Avtar, "naturally we will bear all of them."

"Of course, but I am not one of those who will do things for money, I can tell you very frankly."

"Naturally," protested Ram Avtar, "the thought had not even crossed my mind. But there may be others involved who do not have your moral strength."

"That is quite right," agreed Sharmaji. "Corruption has become root of all evil. But to be very honest, I do not indulge. I am in game only to improve myself. Once I used to also take, but I have made enough. I tell to you as a friend, I am owning three homes and enough other property. Now I will only do to please my friends and improve myself."

'He's repeated that twice,' thought Ram Avtar, 'could he conceivably be serious?'

"But," resumed Sharmaji, "I regard you as friend so I will do and if any damages there are, we can discuss."

"Of course," said Ram Avtar, much relieved, "when?"

"You may come to my office on Monday morning. We will see."

Later at night, Chris thought of the whole scene. He wondered if Sharmaji was actually going to help. Though both the Kapoors seemed optimistic, Chris felt that Sharmaji was not going to do anything without the minister's consent. He had stated this to Ram Avtar after Sharmaji had left.

"Yes," Ram Avtar had agreed, "that will be the main thing."

Chris willed himself into sleep since Kalpana was taking him to see yet another monument the next morning.

Kalpana duly arrived the next day and they set out. Chris wouldn't dream of telling Kalpana, but he was sick to the teeth of monuments in various stages of decay. Everytime he went to one, he stifled a groan. But being with Kalpana had other compensations. Once again they drove to her apartment and made love.

Afterwards, as they lay exhausted, Kalpana asked, "So what do you think of India? You've been here long enough to form an opinion. What characterises it for you?"

"The whine," said Chris promptly. "For the foreigner, there is a persistent drone of hustlers, beggars, conmen. Its a nation of disembodied hands tugging at your sleeve insistently. I get exhausted shaking them off. I mean the national anthem should be the muttered urgings of hustlers. Jeez, I don't think any other country has such a large and diverse variety. But don't you think it's what India does globally, isn't it like one of its own beggars, plucking timidly but persistently at the world's sleeve, wanting, demanding, badgering?"

"I don't think so at all," disagreed Kalpana. "Next you'll be saying I'm like that too."

"Nah, nah," laughed Chris, gathering her into his arms, "I think of you as a great lay, maybe the best in my long and chequered career." He laughed.

Instantly she tensed and drew away from him. Chris could have kicked himself.

"Is that what I am to you?" she demanded, getting out of bed and starting to get into her clothes.

"Hey come back here," protested Chris, "I was just fooling."

In answer she threw his clothes at him. "Let's go," she demanded.

On the drive back Chris kept trying to make up, but Kalpana didn't say a word. When they reached the house she leaned across and opened his door. "At least come in for a drink," urged Chris, but she refused to reply.

Sadly Chris levered himself out of the car and walked through the gate as Kalpana drove away.

"Idiot, idiot, idiot," Chris cursed. "Now you've really gone and done it."

Forlornly he wandered into Mr. Sunder's office.

"Ah good, you are here. I am having lunch. You will have? It is chowmein."

"No thanks. I'm not hungry."

"As you like." Mr. Sunder resumed eating the chowmein, Chris noticed, with his fingers.

Chris sat down, averting his gaze from Mr. Sunder lifting the noodles with his hands and slurping them into his mouth, like a giant mongoose enjoying a plate of snakes.

"You are looking sad," commented Mr. Sunder in between mouthfuls.

"Oh nothing," said Chris, "just some girl problem. You wouldn't know about it."

"Yes, I know. I know about all these things."

"How? I suppose you had an arranged marriage. How would you know?"

"Due to my previous job where I was working."

"What happened there?"

"I was personal secretary to Managing Director. He had lot many girlfriends."

"So how come you got involved?"

"The scoundrel fellow used to dictate to me his love letters to his girlfriends. After three years I said '*Bas baba*.' I cannot tolerate anymore."

40

"Jeez, I don't know what to tell you, except that I've behaved like an animal."

"Never mind," consoled Mr. Sunder, slurping the last of the noodles. "All men may be animals, but all women are animal lovers."

"Thanks a lot," wanly grinned Chris, "But not this one I think. I suspect I've just fumbled the ball. I was right at the goal line and I fumbled."

"Never the mind. We can refer the matter to my friend Rakesh. He is having matrimonial agency. He can find a right person for you."

"Shit no, that's the last thing I need."

"He will do the needful for you as a special case," urged Mr. Sunder, "he is my *langoti yaar.*"

"What?"

"*Langoti yaar.* Underwear friend."

"Whatever. Thanks but no thanks. I'll have to tackle this one on my own."

Chris wandered away, reflecting on what kind of help he had expected from a man who wore white shoes and flared trousers.

Chris couldn't sleep that night, 'Jeez I really screwed up' he told himself. 'The minute I said it, I knew I'd blown it. Damn, damn, damn.' He tossed and turned. Sometime near dawn it occurred to him, 'I must be really keen on her if she can affect me like this. Goddamn.'

4

The next day Chris tried to phone Kalpana. The moment she heard his voice she hung up. He tried again and once more she hung up. Thereafter the number kept coming engaged so she had obviously taken the phone off the hook. Chris got Mr. Sunder to call him a taxi and drove to her apartment. He lumbered his way up the stairs, not wanting to wait for the elevator and rang the door bell. No one answered so he sat on the steps waiting for her to return.

He must have waited for two hours with people brushing past him and staring in curiosity, before he finally gave up. He went down the stairs and found he had no transport to take him home. Finally he waved at a three wheeler scooter that stopped.

"Punjabi Bagh," he said as he struggled to get into the contraption that was clearly too small for him. Finally, sitting sideways he managed to squeeze himself in, with his legs up near his chin, jerking and jolting as the vehicle bounced over every bump on the road, which suddenly seemed to have developed the terrain of a model of the Himalayan range.

It was the most uncomfortable ride of his life and only deepened his savage mood. Whenever the scooter hit a larger bump, his head would hit the curved rod overhead. He tried to look at the road over the driver's shoulder so he could anticipate the bumps and brace himself in advance, but he couldn't seem to spot them. Being twisted like a pretzel didn't help in trying to keep an eye on the road either.

At last the scooter stopped and Chris extricated himself

bit by bit out of the vehicle. He felt like a mechanical toy that could be unscrewed and put together in a different shape.

"Jeez," he grumbled as he paid the scooter driver, "ain't they never heard of football players? Goddamn, the place must be full of pygmies." He hobbled his way into the compound. Hurting physically, in pain emotionally, he creaked his way to his room.

"Goddamn," he cursed himself, 'I never should have said it. But its just a few words, that's all. How do I get her back?'

Just then Ajai Vir walked in. "Say a prayer for us," he told Chris. "We're meeting the minister tomorrow. This is going to be a critical meeting."

"I'll do better than pray," said Chris, "I'll come along if you don't mind. What say?"

Ajay Vir hesitated. "There may be confidential stuff being discussed. I don't know if you'll enjoy it."

"I'll be quiet as a mouse," said Chris. "You won't even notice I'm there. Besides, since we've an agreement on co-operation between your company and ours, I could be useful."

"All right," conceded Ajai Vir, "Maybe you could wait in the reception room."

Ajay Vir went back to his room and found his father there. "So", asked Ram Avtar, "which of the B's should we use this time?"

"That's easy" said Ajay Vir. "We try the Bribery B. What can we offer?"

"Bribery means different things to different people. One man's food is another's poison. What I mean is that we must find out his weaknesses and pamper him there. So keep your ears open about anything he says which might reveal his weakness. Also you are to talk to people among his party workers as to what they know about his likes and dislikes. Also go meet your friends in the press who might know some more about him."

"OK Dad. But Chris wants to come with us. I've told him he can come but he'll have to wait in the reception room. Is that fine?"

"Yes, that's fine, but don't discuss money with him. They're our collaborators, but a lot of things have to be kept away from them. Do you understand?"

"Yes Dad. But what sort of things?"

"I have been meaning to tell you, and now you have to know. They've given us a very good deal — in all areas, because they think we're a smaller company than is the case. We sent them our balance sheet, but as you well know that is very inaccurate. If Stark Industries ever discovered the real size of our company, there would be great inconvenience for us. So keep Chris busy in things other than the business. Make sure he's happy but out of our way. Is that clear?"

"Sure Dad," agreed Ajai Vir.

"Good, let's sleep early today, because tomorrow could be critical."

The next morning Ram Avtar woke early and looked with seriousness at his wife's photograph. He sat before the print and spoke to it.

"We're facing a crisis and I wish I had you to support me. Ajay Vir is too raw to handle this. Sometimes I feel it was wrong to send him to America to study Business Management. Perhaps I should have kept him here and taught him how a business is actually run. Right now he thinks only of millions of dollars and huge expansion plans. He has to learn that it is also wise to grow slowly so you can digest whatever you're swallowing.

Now he has to learn how to cope with scoundrels like Sevak Chand. Lets see how the day goes. It could be crucial for us. I hope your blessings are on our family."

After breakfast, Chris, Ram Avtar and Ajay Vir got into the chauffeur-driven Mercedes and set off to the Ministry.

Chris looked at the masses of flowers blossoming everywhere, green trees swaying in the breeze, the delicious feel of the sun caressing the face and he wondered how ugliness could happen on such a beautiful day as this.

They passed by the majestic India Gate.

"I've often wondered," said Chris, "what's that for."

"It commemorates the Indian soldiers who died in World War I."

"Indians fought in World War I?" asked Chris in surprise." I didn't know that."

"Who do you think won their wars for the British?" grunted Ram Avtar. "It just proves that they couldn't win any war unless they had someone to do the fighting for them."

They turned into the Ministry's entrance, drove down a little and stopped. They got out of the car, walked up the stairs and to the reception. A queue had formed there, but they tried to bypass it and went directly to the counter. Two men sat behind, surrounded by telephones and registers.

"Appointment with the Minister", said Ajai Vir.

Both the men ignored them.

"Appointment with the Minister," said Ajai Vir more loudly.

One of the men looked up. "Gentleman," he said "kindly wait in the line. Your turn will come."

Grumbling, they went to the end of the queue. The line inched forward as they waited impatiently.

"Can't we tell him the appointment's for 11?" asked Chris. "Its very nearly that."

Ajay Vir shrugged helplessly. At last they reached the counter. Ram Avtar began to fill a register but was stopped by one of the men.

"Kindly call Sharmaji and confirm. Your name is not on my list of people to see the Minister. You may have to try on Sharmaji's extension."

Ram Avtar patiently tried the number. It rang but no one picked it up.

"He's not in," said Ram Avtar.

"Then kindly wait."

"But we have confirmed appointment with the Minister."

"I am not doubting, but rules are rules. Without intimation I cannot allow. Please wait."

"But what about our appointment?"

"That is there, but I cannot issue chit without sanction."

Seething, the trio huddled together. One of the receptionists beckoned Ram Avtar.

"The gentleman with you, is he a foreigner?"

"Obviously," and Ram Avtar.

"Then I think he is needing Home Ministry sanction to enter this Ministry."

"Shit," swore Ajay Vir. "Don't be ridiculous. We can't possibly get that today."

"Rules are rules," countered the man.

Ram Avtar was looking thoughtful. "Home Ministry, you say?" he enquired.

"Yes."

"Perhaps also the Finance Ministry."

"Dad," burst out Ajai Vir, "have you gone nuts?"

Ram Avtar waved him to silence.

"The Finance Ministry?" he enquired again.

"That is upto you," responded the man. "But it may be lot more botheration for you."

"Not at all," reassured Ram Avtar, "after all I am also giving you trouble."

"No, no," protested the receptionist, "I am only doing job."

"That I can see," admired Ram Avtar, "you are doing it very well too. And so many people are giving you trouble. Some consideration has to be there. Can I have a word with you in private?"

"No need, no need," protested the man weakly as he got up with alacrity.

Just then Ajay Vir spotted Sharmaji crossing the lobby.

Sharmaji saw them and understood the situation perfectly.

"Why are you not issuing gate pass?" he demanded.

"Just filling in sir," said the receptionist, not looking Ram Avtar in the eye.

Bearing the precious scraps of paper, they marched triumphantly to the elevators. It was surprisingly clean and unblemished by graffitti. They stopped at a floor where a saffron coloured carpet extended to the elevator entrance. They walked down the corridor and into Sharmaji's room.

This was fairly spartan, with a sofa against the wall and chairs scattered around the table. This was piled high with files that looked so sturdily like a part of the table, that they may have been natural life forms that over the years had grown and grown till they reached their current formidable size.

Sharmaji seated himself and could be discerned in a gap between the files. He pushed a buzzer on his table.

"Four teas," he ordered the peon who opened the door, "and no sugar in mine."

The bearer exited and Sharmaji addressed Ram Avtar. "I am sorry for the delay downstairs. What to do? These rascals at reception do no work at all, but we cannot remove them. How to manage I do not know."

"That is quite all right," said Ram Avtar. "At least we are here. But I am worried because we are late. I hope the Minister is not busy with some other appointment."

"Not to worry," said Sharmaji, "I will do needful. But speaking frankly, there may be some problem with regards to Chrisji. The Minister has not been informed that there is an international presence here."

"Hey, no problem," said Chris. "I'll just sit here. You guys go ahead."

Just then a red light that was on over the door went off and a green one came on.

"That is signal for us," said Sharmaji getting to his feet. Ram Avtar and Ajai Vir also got up hastily.

"Good luck," said Chris giving Ajai Vir a thumbs up sign as they trooped out of the door.

Chris settled himself in his chair and began to read one of the newspapers lying on the table. It was a fairly long wait. He tried not to think of Kalpana and had finished reading two newspapers by the time the Kapoors and Sharmaji returned. The father and son were jubilant, but Sharmaji looked thoughtful.

"So its done," said Ram Avtar. "We will do our end and you may kindly do from your end."

Sharmaji nodded distractedly.

"Many thanks for your kindness. We could not do without the trouble you have taken. Let the matter be solved and we will look after you," said Ram Avtar.

Sharmaji grunted and Chris felt his heart sink, but the Kapoors were too delighted to notice anything amiss.

"We will take your leave then," said Ram Avtar. And in a flurry of handshakes they left.

As soon as they got into the car, Chris asked, "What happened?"

"We lucked out. Sevak Chand agrees with us that the strike is wrong and should be stopped," said Ajay Vir. "He said 'Nehruji said industries were the modern temples of India and need to be protected.' So some of the labourers who don't want to strike will be encouraged by us to come back to work. If Prabal Kumar tries to stop them, the police will have been instructed by Sharmaji speaking on behalf of Sevak Chand to give them full protection and make sure they get to work. Once the workers see that the others are working, they'll break ranks and the strike will be over."

"Hey, time out," said Chris, "it can't be as easy as that. Supposing none of the workers agree to go to work. What then?"

"We'll make them an offer," grinned Ajay Vir, "as the great Godfather said, that they can't refuse."

And so they did. Lal Verma went to the homes of some of the workers, stepping distastefully over garbage and foul liquids that slithered through the slum where they lived. He asked the way to their shanties and was directed wonderingly by people who had never seen a sahib come visiting their dismal hovels. Behind him walked an assistant carrying an enormous shopping bag and on either side walked two large men with bulges under their shirts.

49

Chris had been sent along by Ram Avtar, ostensibly to let him see genuine poverty, but also, as he advised Chris, to let him keep an eye on Verma who might offer some money to the workers, come back and claim he had given them twice as much and pocket the difference.

Chris looked around in horror. The shacks were made of sack and wood. Some had no doors and he could see the interiors with just rolled beddings in them and a few plates. The stench of urine, excreta and decaying junk made it impossible for him to breathe. He put a handkerchief over his nose and took short breaths. The ground underneath felt slushy and he dared not look at what he was stepping on. He felt entombed in a cocoon of unbearable smells. 'This must be what hell is like,' he thought desperately.

But gradually as he got used to the smell, his eyes began to clear and he started to notice something odd. There was the laughter of children at every corner. They had taken old bicycle tyres and were rolling them along the ground, others were playing unfamiliar games using stones and balls. The men were wary but helpful. None looked like they were in distress, much less starving.

'Jeez,' thought Chris, 'with such misery all around, how come they're not sad? It'd have created a revolution in the States.' He reflected further. 'It must be the vote,' he concluded. 'They are happy because they have the vote.'

By now he was beginning to see beyond the obvious, overwhelming poverty. Intermingled with the sound of laughing children, he heard Hindi music everywhere. 'They can afford radios,' he thought in astonishment. But when he looked up accidentally at the roofs he gaped. There was a scattering of television aerials poised casually on several roofs. Such symbols of the middle class life in this cemetery of human

50

hopes was like seeing a neon McDonald's sign glowing in the middle of a graveyard.

'Jeez,' gasped Chris in bafflement, stepping hugely over an artistically composed pile of shit. 'Nothing in this country is what it seems.' He looked back at the squiggles of excreta. They looked too contrived, as though there had been a pre-determined pattern to their excretion. 'Maybe its a form of art among India's poor,' began to suspect Chris. 'Maybe they can make landscapes and portraits out of it. Who knows in this country? Maybe I can send one to Mom to hang in the living room. What a hit it'd be in Tulsa.'

They reached a hut where apparently one of the workers lived. He came out, observed them calmly, recognised Verma and invited them in courteously. Chris squeezed painfully through the door. He found a small room, scrupulously clean with various belongings stacked neatly in their place. 'If he can keep his own house so clean, why the hell doesn't he clear up the garbage and stuff outside?" groused Chris to himself.

They had seated themselves and the worker's wife, her face covered with the sari, was busy making tea at one end of the room over an earthen stove set in the ground. At the other end of the room a black and white TV set was on, though the sound had been turned off. With a feeling of rising incredulousness, Chris saw the programme was a Bugs Bunny show. On top of the TV lay small religious idols and pictures of Hindu gods and goddesses.

'Jesus,' wondered Chris, 'does he pray to them when the TV is on? What if its a Hindi song show, whose dancers look like a Las Vegas chorus line suddenly overcome by nymphomania? Anyway,' he reasoned, 'from what I hear, Hindu gods and goddesses are pretty cool dudes and quite

51

likely to look on the gyrations of their worshippers very tolerantly, if not actually approvingly.'

After all, many of them were no mean dancers themselves. In fact, Mr. Sunder had once explained to him, the Lord of Creation had danced the universe into being and on the day of destruction he would dance it out of existence. 'Why can't our own Jesus Christ do that?' thought Chris suddenly feeling inferior. 'Get off that old cross and do a little tap dance. Something to turn on the crowds.'

His heretical reverie was interrupted when the worker, who had gone out, returned. He spoke briefly to Verma, the shopping bag was opened and bound wads of rupee notes taken out and given to a queue of people who came into the hut, gathered their notes and left. Chris sipped his tea, which was very milky and very sweet and watched the nearly unending procession. Finally the last man counted his notes painfully, licking his thumb periodically, and then left.

"Its done," said Verma with satisfaction, "About a quarter of the company's workers live in this colony and they have all agreed. Sethji will be pleased. Let us leave."

Chris squeezed out of the hut and the stench leapt at him.

"How do we know," he asked Verma, "that the workers won't just keep the money and refuse to return to work?"

Verma gestured at the two heavily built men behind them. "The workers know we'd return again and this time with more of these gentlemen. It would not be wise of them at all."

"So when do they start work?"

"Tomorrow morning. Sharmaji will have instructed the police. Let us see how Prabal Kumar stops us now."

5

The night was a nerve wracking one.

Prabal Kumar had heard of Verma's visit and its success and Mr. Kapoor received word that he would be sending a gang of toughs to ensure that the bought over workers did not enter the factory.

"Dad," asked Ajai Vir as Jingle Bells rang out repeatedly and a veritable rainbow of lights flashed, "shouldn't we also get some guys to add muscle to our workers? I mean they are no match for the kind of goons Prabal can produce."

"No need," said Ram Avtar, gulping his whisky. "I have spoken to Sharmaji and requested him to do the needful."

"What did he say?" asked Chris.

"Nothing. But in the government you know these things are not discussed openly on phone. But Mantriji has said 'Nehruji called factories the temples of modern India and they need to be protected.' Sharmaji will take the hint. It is a clear *ishara*."

"Sir," asked Verma tentatively, "I may not ask this but I hope Mantriji and Sharmaji are ... er, um ... having our gratitude expressed to them in concrete terms."

"No," laughed Ram Avtar, his face now flushed, "that is the greatest fun. Mantriji has his own reasons for humiliating Prabal Kumar and Sharmaji says he now has made so much money that he only wants to improve himself." He laughed hugely. "So long as it improves us also, why we should object?" He roared with laughter. "Now *beta*," he told Ajai Vir, "reconfirm with your journalist friends,

53

particularly photographers, that they will be there. The workers going into the factory must be splashed in all the papers. It will be such a humiliation for Prabal that he will be destroyed and that is what the Minister wants. Please call the journalists early in the morning, you know how late they sleep. Have the crates of Scotch been sent?"

"Of course Dad... They're on their way."

"Even more reason to call them early then. Don't forget. Now lets go to bed, we have a tiring day tomorrow."

Chris tossed and turned most of the night in excitement. It was like the night before a big game, with its hopes for victory, its fear of defeat and the horror of injury. He would have enjoyed the anticipation, particularly since the alcohol they had been consuming all evening in celebration had dulled his fears, but his heart still ached thinking of Kalpana.

'Jeez,' he sat up in bed, his legs drawn up. 'I'm such an asshole. Why'd I say a stupid thing like that? Shit,' he lamented to himself, 'it was going great. We were perfect together, oh shit, oh shit,' he crouched over his legs. 'Anyway,' he sighed, 'maybe its just as well. She's getting married to Ajai Vir and if word ever got out the stuff would really hit the fan. Boy howdy. That would really be something. Its the last time Dad would let me do anything. Its really just sensible that I stay away from her.'

Thus consoled, he slid back and tried to sleep.

Ten minutes later he called Mr. Sunder on the in-house telecom. Given the importance of the next twenty four hours, Mr. Sunder had put himself on non-stop duty.

"Good morning sir," he said to Chris, "You are needing something?"

"Just your company," said Chris. "I know its 2 in the morning, but there's something I want to talk to you about."

There was a pause. "I am understanding sir," Mr. Sunder's voice could barely suppress the excitement, "I am coming at once."

And he did.

"Get a drink," Chris waved him towards the bathroom. "You do drink?"

"Well sir, not usually sir, but today being special......." He trailed away to the bathroom and Jingle Bells could be heard for a very long time.

He returned holding a tall glass full of whisky and wiped his hands on his bell bottoms. He seated himself on a chair and gulped down half the glass. He smiled tentatively at Chris.

"I think I am knowing," he hiccuped gently.

"Yeah?" said Chris in alarm, "Does everyone know?"

"No, no, no, no," soothed Mr. Sunder. "It is being between us sir."

"Phew," breathed Chris in relief. "I thought I'd ruined everything."

Mr. Sunder shook his head sagely, smiling in pleasure.

"It is all safe with me sir." He slid a little on the chair.

"Well," asked Chris, "what do you think I should do?"

Mr. Sunder took a long drink from his glass, which was beginning to waver, as was his voice.

"As I am saying," slurred Mr. Sunder and it dawned on Chris that this was not his first drink of the evening. "As I am saying ..." and then the lights went out suddenly.

There was a startled silence as they adjusted to the darkness in a suddenly unfamiliar room.

"Well shit," recovered Chris, "if that happened in the summer you'd really fry."

"So what?" roared Mr. Sunder, startling Chris. "At least its a public sector power cut. I am enjoying like anything. I am telling to you sir, this liberalisation will be finishing India. Finishing. Now, at least they are our own public sector power cuts. I am saying to you, we will be slaves again. Slaves of Coca Cola. I am hearing that no more milk for our children, only Pepsi. I am saying," Mr. Sunder's voice rose to a drunken crescendo, shrieking, "will Indian women now having Pepsi cans instead of breasts?"

The lights came on, catching Mr. Sunder half up, frozen with his glass held unsteadily above him. Slowly he tumbled back into his chair, his glass now empty.

"Well, India is finished because of these bloody politician fellows I tell you. Liberalisation," he grumbled.

"Well yeah, right," groped Chris trying to steer the conversation back subtly. "What do I do about, you know, my problem?"

Mr. Sunder lurched to his feet. "No problem," he gloated. "No one is knowing. Give it to me. Not for me, naturally, you are understanding, you are understanding. Only for my friends. For sociological reasons."

Chris was aghast, "Give her to your friends. Hey man, get real. She won't even talk to me no more. Why the fuck should I give her to your friends?"

"Her," pondered Mr. Sunder staggering a little. "Who her?"

Chris considered this in perplexity. "My girl friend. Or, well, you know, whatever. What the hell are you talking about?"

"Playboy magazine," responded Mr. Sunder. "You are having girl friend?"

"Get out of here," ordered Chris in some dudgeon. "Some guru you are."

Mr. Sunder got out of there, reeling from furniture to furniture.

Chris sighed even more. "Horny son of a bitch," he muttered. "But then," he had to admit after a moment's thought, "so am I."

On an impulse he dragged the phone and punched Kalpana's number. It rang and rang and he was about to put it down when she picked up her phone.

"Hello," said her sleepy voice.

"Jeez," exulted Chris, his heart racing. Of all the sounds in this wide world, nothing beats the sleepy hello of the woman you love just waking up.

"Don't put it down," breathed Chris, "don't hang up. At least let me say what I gotta say."

"Hello," she said again, her voice stronger, recognising him. "Chris, is that you? Whats wrong? Is something the matter? What time is it? Has anything happened there?"

"No, its okay," Chris tried to pacify her, "its just me. I want to, like, you know, just say hello."

"At nearly three in the morning?" Her voice had calmed down and was even starting to sound amused. "So okay. You've said your hello."

"No, wait, hang on," demanded Chris. "I wanted to, you know, like, you know what I mean, apologise for what I said and stuff. You know. Okay?"

"Humm Okay. You've said your sorries. Now go to sleep."

"Does this mean I can, you know, like , see you again? I mean, no funny stuff, I promise. Just friends."

"We'll see," she said. "Not any time soon. I need to think."

"Okay," rapidly agreed Chris. "Anything you like. I didn't mean any harm with what I said. I mean I don't always manage to say what I mean. I mean I think pretty good, but I don't talk too great. Know what I mean?"

There was a muffled sound from the other side.

"I mean we'll do whatever you say, OK? Whatever you want. So what would you like?"

Her voice was a little kinder. "Chris, I would like very much at this point to go to sleep."

"Sure," agreed Chris with alacrity. "But can I at least, like you know, call you again?"

"We'll see," she said. "Try." And the line went dead.

Gently Chris replaced the receiver on the cradle. "Yay," he pumped his fist in the air. " 'Try,' she said. 'Try.' All right."

He was asleep by the time his head hit the pillow.

The next day didn't go as well for any of them. They had driven out of Punjabi Bagh at six in the morning in the Mercedes. Chris, despite two hours of sleep, felt happier than he ever felt before. At that time of the morning the Ring Road was deserted and the powerful car made good time. As they flashed past familiar landmarks, Chris could barely recognise them devoid of the dust and fumes and angrily honking cars that usually encased them. 'Cities are like women,' mused Chris. 'They change from hour to hour, season to season. They absorb their surroundings and they reflect it. And as that changes, so do they. You wake up with one woman in the morning, encounter a different one at work, a third specimen cooks dinner for the kids and a completely different one goes out dancing with you at night. Men, on the other hand,' he thought with contempt, 'were such ... what was an apt description ... such predictable pricks. They came in two varieties, if even that, hard and soft. Women,' he concluded, 'were so much more fun to know. If they were being nice to you of course,' he hastily ended this chain of thought.

They had entered the great industrial belt linking Delhi to Faridabad and though Chris thought such a diversity of factories was great for India, he wondered whose bright idea it was to place them so close to the capital city. You were guaranteed pollution, not just with the factories and the power stations, but with the armies of workers and managers in their buses and cars and scooters and motorcycles, not to mention the trucks carrying in goods and carrying out finished products. With so many jobs around, you were also certain to attract an endless stream of job seekers who would inevitably settle in the city and add to its population problems. 'I bet,' thought Chris with some pride, 'I'm the only football player in American history to worry about the population problems of Third World countries. Sometimes, I really wonder,' he mused for not the first time, 'if I hadn't become a football player and spent my entire childhood and college years on the field getting my brains hit out of me, I might actually have got an education, developed my mind and been able to express all these ideas knocking around but... now I'm just another football player who never really got educated or was taught anything and was pushed up every year to the next grade like in all the other schools and colleges to keep the football coaches happy. Good thing my dad's got a business, otherwise like all the other guys who never made it to the professional league, I'd have been a salesman for some company making women's underwear. And boy, the stories I've heard about ex-football players and the housewives they meet to sell lingerie to ...'

Before he could ruminate on these stories, the car slowed and turned off the highway towards the KapCo plant. The workers were there blocking the road, some sitting, some still asleep, but they all got out of the way to let the car pass. They recognised Ram Avtar and involuntarily some of them touched their forehead. Others looked away embarrassed, a few glared angrily.

The guards opened the gates and the car drove into the grounds and up to the main building. They got out and went up in the elevator to the second floor, to the manager's dining room whose full length windows looked onto the grounds and over the wall into the world outside. They pulled up chairs and sat looking through the glass in silence.

The workers had regrouped on the road and were talking among themselves. Prabal Kumar's car arrived.

"All quiet so far," commented Ram Avtar. "Ajai, when are the loyal workers expected?"

"In fifteen minutes Dad. We've organised three buses for them. They should be arriving soon."

Lal Verma entered through the swing doors behind them just then. "Look sir," he pointed in excitement, "the police have arrived. Sharmaji has done the needful."

Four police trucks slowly trundled off the highway and then drove alongside the factory wall before stopping about a hundred yards away from the workers. The backs of the trucks opened and the policemen began to leap out wearing helmets and carrying wicker shields and lathis.

"They don't look too tough," said Chris dubiously.

"That's deceptive," disagreed Ram Avtar, "when they charge with those sticks, I've seen them clear howling mobs of thousands."

"But they're not even armed," objected Chris.

"The last truck is," said Verma. "The men are still inside but they are carrying rifles and tear gas guns. I overtook them while I was on my way."

"So they mean business," exulted Ajai Vir. "Shall we

open a bottle of champagne to celebrate the end of Prabal Kumar's career?"

"Lets wait for it to the end first," cautioned Ram Avtar, but even he couldn't resist smiling. "And here are our journalist friends," he gestured.

Then the workers from the buses, still shouting slogans, began to move towards the workers blocking their path. They came face to face and the slogan shouting on both sides intensified. Soon they began to push and scuffle sporadically, but other than gesticulate at each other threateningly, nothing serious happened.

Suddenly, perhaps inevitably, one of the workers, no one could tell which side he belonged to, fell down, his mouth bleeding. Enraged, both sides began to swing at each other.

"Not to worry sir," said Verma, "our men among them are carrying short sticks. They'll sort these people out."

Verma's workers could actually be seen ploughing through the mob, like a liner through turbulent seas, almost upto the car where Prabal Kumar stood. Just when it looked as if they would break through and stream into the factory gates, Prabal Kumar looked at the shamiana and raised his hand.

With hoarse shrieks that they could all hear in the dining room, a group of men came racing out, carrying lathis and iron rods. They crashed into the group around Prabal and as his workers hastily ran to the side, the armed men began to pulverise the workers Verma had hired. Blood and flesh flew, the workers screamed, but they had nowhere to go because Prabal's men had blocked one side, while his thugs were howling and slashing on the other.

"The police," shouted Ram Avtar, "Why doesn't the bloody police charge?"

61

Verma ran down the steps, through the grounds and leapt up the wall next to the police line.

"Charge," he shouted, oblivious of the glass pieces on top of the wall imbedding into his forearms, "are you blind? Don't you see what is happening? For God's sake why don't you charge?" he pleaded.

The policeman nearest to him shook head. "We have no orders yet sir"

"I am giving you the orders," shrieked Verma in tears, "don't you see what's happening to them?"

"Only the inspector can order sir".

"Where is the inspector?" pleaded Verma.

"In the truck, on the wireless, getting orders from Delhi."

"Please say I am begging him ," beseeched Verma. "Have you no humanity? See, my people are getting killed. They have wives and children like you. At least fire the tear gas."

The policeman was regretful but firm. "No orders sir. The inspector will order us. And Delhi will order him."

Verma fell back from the wall, his arms bloody, his spectacles askew.

From their vantage point in the dining room, the group watched in anguish and horror as the slaughter below continued. Soon, except for a few who had managed to run back in the direction they had come from, the rest lay writhing and screaming in agony as Prabal's men used their rods and lathis to methodically break their bones, avoiding their heads, necks and groin.

Above them, on the hood, arms akimbo, a stern look on that baby face, stood Prabal Kumar. Finally, he raised a hand. "Stop," he commanded, "enough has been done." His minions paused, panting from their exertions, their clothes streaked with blood and gore.

"Go," Prabal gestured to them once again, "you have done well." His butchers shambled back, flicking the flesh sticking to their weapons.

"Look," ordered Prabal to the group of workers who had frozen with fear and horror at the massacre of their colleagues. "See the strength of Prabal Kumar. And remember that this is your strength too. Let your *maalik* see what happens to those who betray the workers. Let him now come and talk to us about our just demands. I think today we have corrected his senses. What do we want?" he roared, trying to raise a slogan from the crowd.

The answer was a ragged whisper.

"What do we want?" he demanded again.

The answer was even more muted.

Prabal Kumar leapt off the car. "Have no fear," he assured the workers before getting into the car with his assistants. "I am with you. And while I am there nobody can do anything to you and all your demands will be met. Jai Hind."

The car door slammed and he drove off.

6

The drive back to Delhi was in stunned silence. Ram Avtar had turned grey and looked twenty years older. Ajai Vir had vomitted twice and had tears in his eyes. Chris was shell shocked.

The buses that had brought in the workers had been used to carry them to a nearby hospital, Lal Verma lying among them. The police had helped in carrying the workers to the buses and then got back into their trucks and left.

Ram Avtar had the chauffeur drive them straight to the Ministry. All three of them went up the stairs and brushed past the reception and the guard and began to climb. The guard considered chasing after them, but he had seen their faces and decided against it.

All three barged into Sharmaji's office and seated themselves. Sharmaji had been dictating a letter to his secretary, but seeing them come in motioned for him to leave.

"Ah, here you are," he said pleasantly. "I have been expecting you. Some tea perhaps?"

"Why?" asked Ram Avtar quietly but furiously. "Why did you do this?"

Sharmaji spread his arms apologetically. "I was helpless."

"The minister asked this?" demanded Ajai Vir menacingly.

Sharmaji looked at him sharply. "Ministers never ask such things," he said warningly.

"Then why," asked Ram Avtar, his spectacles shining

with the spirit that had brought him so far in his trek through life, "why did you allow all this to happen? You heard the minister. He said clearly that as per Nehruji's wishes, factories were the temples of modern India and must be protected."

Sharmaji nodded. "And so it was, the factory."

"Fat lot of protection," burst in Ajai Vir "Do you know how many people are crippled for life?"

"The minister did not mention about protecting the workers. He mentioned, as per Nehruji's wishes, about protecting the factory. This was done. That is what the police were there for," Sharmaji said shortly.

"And what made you think," asked Ram Avtar with barely suppressed fury, "that when the minister mentioned about protecting the factory, he did not include the workers in it?"

"Because," said Sharmaji patiently, as one would when explaining the obvious to a child, "when the minister mentioned about protecting the factory, the minister did not smile."

There was an utter silence.

Then both Chris and Ajai Vir rose in wrath to their feet. Ram Avtar gestured repeatedly to them to sit down.

"I would like," he said with a gentleness matching Sharmaji's, "to have the honour of an audience with the minister sahib."

Sharmaji began to look apologetic. "Unfortunately, due to prior ..."

Ram Avtar rose to his feet, raising his hand to stop Sharmaji. "At once," he said "At once." What he left unsaid but which hung like a Damoclean guillotine's blade suspended by the thinnest of hair in the air was the fact that as a large contributor to political parties and a heavy advertiser in the media, he had the influence to make life decidedly difficult for Sharmaji and his master, if he were pushed too far and if he stopped caring about the consequences.

Keenly aware of all that Ram Avtar had left unsaid, Sharmaji sighed deeply, thought for a moment, then left the room.

He returned soon. "Despite his tight schedule," he began, "but given the tragic events of this morning ..."

By then they had brushed past him into the minister's chamber.

It was a vast room, with a sofa set at one end and a huge semicircle table at the other, behind which reposed Sevak Chand, all seven feet and 100 lbs of him. His chin was on his chest as he watched them approach him.

'He looks like a vulture watching a potential victim,' thought Chris.

But he greeted them respectfully, with a reverential *namaste*, his eyes on Chris.

"A foreign visitor," he said, sizing up Chris. "Indiraji used to always say," his eyes flickered probingly to Ram Avtar, "welcome a tourist and send back a friend."

Given the events of the morning, Chris thought this unlikely, but he let it pass.

Ram Avtar understood. "Mr. Stark is our foreign collaborator visiting us and a witness to the events of this morning."

Sevak Chand began to look positively alarmed. "As the Prime Minister himself has repeatedly said, foreign collaborations are most welcome and will bring prosperity to both parties and our great countries. However," he looked under hooded eyes at Ram Avtar, "the PM has also made it explicitly plain, both through personal interviews and in statements to Parliament itself, that the entire matter involving the entry of the foreign media is a separate issue and involves delicate matters requiring perhaps an expert committee to be set up. He has categorically stated," he queried Ram Avtar, "that not only has no decision been taken on this complex question with ramifications on our national security, but the matter has not even been discussed by the full cabinet."

"Mr. Stark's family," placated Ram Avtar, sensing the danger flags flying, "makes plastic buckets. They have nothing to do with the media."

Sevak Chand relaxed. "Indiraji herself, I am told," he encouraged Chris, "had ordered that plastic buckets be used when washing clothes in her house instead of iron buckets. Though of course," he added hastily, horrified at this indiscretion his relief had caused, "I am too small a man to know this by myself. But I hear these things," he gestured towards Ram Avtar, "from friends and well wishers like you."

The blame having been securely laid on others, he leaned back.

Ram Avtar had not been aware that he had been a well wisher of the minister and particularly did not feel like one at this moment.

"Minister," he leaned forward, "there has been a murderous attack on my workers and on the outskirts of your very own constituency. I am protesting in the strongest possible terms. I am not opposed to unions. I think both management and workers benefit from them, but Mr. Prabal Kumar's methods are violent and vicious. They are unacceptable in a democratic society. Scores of my workers have been maimed for life. I ask that Mr. Kumar be arrested and brought to trial as an instigator of the attack and an accomplice. I demand that justice be done and union goondaism be eliminated sir."

Sevak Chand's half-closed eyes drooped even lower. "I have only just now been informed of the sad events of the day and will be issuing a statement to the press strongly condemning violence which is counter to our glorious heritage and against the teachings of the great gurus, Hindu, Muslim and Sikh. The PM too has hinted at his opposition to violence and Gandhiji himself once said, 'Let us eschew violence.' Gandhiji ..." He paused, looking at Chris.

"You are American?" he asked.

Chris nodded.

"The Father of our nation," he explained to Chris. "An extremely great man." His eyes closed as his careful mind examined whether this viewpoint could be twisted by his enemies to get him into trouble. He decided it couldn't, but thought why risk it. "Off the record of course," he added as a precaution.

He resumed, "Gandhiji would have been shocked and in this year which would have been the 125th of his life, I think it appropriate to issue an appeal..." His eyes closed again as his mind meticulously ticked, "to add my name to an appeal," he amended, "to be issued by Padmashree, Arjuna award winners and individuals highly placed in society, including the Lions Club, to pursue the path of non-violence as advocated by Gandhiji."

He stopped.

Believing he must be thinking further, they waited. After a while he added. "Thank you for your kind visit and making time for me in your crowded schedule."

Ajai Vir rose in stunned outrage. "That's all? What about all those battered workers? What about the attack? Will Prabal Kumar get away with this? And all you're going to do is issue an appeal?"

"The law will naturally take its own course. Rajivji often said, 'Nobody howsoever mighty is above the law.' " It suddenly occurred to Sevak Chand that this might be construed to be a hint about that painful Bofors business, so he quickly added, "thereby, showing his firm faith in secularism which is enshrined in our Constitution and reflected in all the great religions of India and for which he laid down his life, and Mrs. Gandhi too, for the unity, integrity and prosperity of India to which the Congress is completely wedded, as revealed in the manifesto released in the Tirupati session of the Congress, which was attended by the rank and file of the Party which gained freedom for our nation, which is a fact that cannot be disputed by even the taunts of the opposition parties whose role in the independence struggle has now been exposed to the world."

This of course threw all those listening into complete confusion as it was intended to.

"But what's going to be done?" plaintively demanded Ajai Vir.

Sevak Chand looked evilly at him for asking such a distasteful question, decided it was too dangerous to answer and said nothing.

"Now look," said Ajai Vir, his voice rising, "Minister or not, your Mr. Sharmaji knew this was going to happen. Aren't you at least going to arrest that bastard Prabal Kumar?"

The minister had turned into a stone statue. Behind Ajai Vir there was a rustle and they turned to find to their surprise that Sharmaji had been standing there all along.

"A magisterial enquiry will be initiated," Sharmaji assured them soothingly "and as per its recommendations, action will be taken to the fullest extent of the law."

"When?" demanded Ajai Vir.

"As soon as it gives in the report."

"When will it give the report?"

"After it has been set up."

"When will it be set up?"

"With all possible speed, as per the rules and regulations of the Government of India as amended from time to time by the competent authority."

"When?" insisted Ajai Vir in frustrations. "Give me a damn date."

"The Government of India," Sharmaji rebuked sternly, "does not believe in the concept of dates. Neither," he said stingingly, "in giving them, nor," he added contemptuously "in adhering to them. It will happen when it will happen."

"And meanwhile," persisted a furious Ajai Vir, his face flushed, "if Prabal Kumar arrives again and decides to tear down the factory, will you rebuild it for us?" he asked Sharmaji bitingly. He was really beyond all control. "Mantriji, its your responsibility," Ajai Vir foamed, "don't keep shoving it at this senile idiot. You tell us. Tell us specifically. What the hell are you going to do to protect our factory, to prevent violence, to break the strike? Tell me. Tell me now, in front of this fat man."

There was a total and disbelieving silence. Sharmaji glared, his face beaded in sweat. The minister was so still that it appeared as though his spirit had ascended into astral layers leaving behind a lifeless shell. Ram Avtar was immobile but alert. 'Way to go,' thought Chris in pain, wondering if there were any chairs in any ministry designed to accommodate football players.

"Well? Well?" demanded Ajay Vir in fury. "Speak to me. I'm entitled to an answer. I'm not asking you for any damn favour. Its your job to protect us. That's what we pay you a salary for. Now I want to know right now. How are you going to protect us? Do you know the sort of things I've seen today? Now either I get a straight answer from you right now", Ajay Vir was panting, "or I'm going to call Ramu in New York. I was in Xavier's with him. I'll go personally to Shobhana, to Aroon. A.N. Verma is going to hear of this attack this very evening." He was nearly shrieking.

With each name, Sevak Chand's eyes had flickered, as though each proper noun was an urgent fax message recalling his soul to earth from wherever it had gone.

He began to breathe visibly again, a sign that he had fully returned and his eyes were fixed completely on Ajai Vir, still on his feet, sweating and panting. Nothing could be read in those hooded orbs, but obviously, the machinery behind was whirring, taking in the distraught young man in front, his silent though formidable father, the names the young man had flung and whether he actually knew them....... which he probably did, thought the minister .... how far they would go on his behalf........ probably not very far, concluded Sevak Chand, but then who could say .... and the explosive potential of the whole situation, particularly with liberalisation underway and the state elections around the corner. There were other considerations too, but no one at that time could have been aware that they were in Sevak Chand's mind. He came to a decision with astonishing speed.

"Sharmaji," he barked and all four were startled at the sudden authority rampant in his voice. "Ensure full security to the factory. Take all measures to protect the Kapoor family, their residence and all present. No threat must be allowed to occur to them or to their lives. Monitor the situation personally." His voice turned even sharper as he looked

71

directly at Sharmaji, his whole body radiating a power quite bewilderingly at odds with his normal, crouched, brooding insouciance. "Do you understand?" he rapped.

"Yes sir," supplicated Sharmaji, bowing and edging backwards and imploringly summoning the others with his hand.

They rose too, muttering their thanks and moving out. In the corridor Sharmaji whirled around, strode furiously to his room and slammed the door shut.

By the time Ram Avtar's Mercedes returned to their Punjabi Bagh residence, they found policemen armed with rifles at the gate and clumps of others in position all around the house. Some were pitching a tent just outside the wall where they obviously planned to stay for a while. A message from the factory said that several dozen policemen had similarly arrived there and were on guard at every conceivable approach and were patrolling the walls.

Chris whistled as they walked into the house. "So they can move fast when they want to," he said. "Its touch down time. And you did it boy," he thumped Ajai Vir on the back who grinned awkwardly. "Just lost my cool with the fuckers, that's all," Ajai Vir muttered embarrassedly.

"Well, lets go get drunk boy," enthused Chris. "Its party time. May be we could go get Kalpana and hit a disco or something."

Ajai Vir looked for permission to his father who was seated in his favourite chair and seemed lost in thought.

"What say Dad?" he asked. "Can we go paint the town red?"

Ram Avtar shook his head. "No," he said shortly, "It hasn't ended. I think its just begun."

"Come on Dad," Ajay Vir tried to cheer him up. "Don't be such a pessimist. You heard the minister. And you've seen

72

the cops. Have you ever known the Government to act so fast when they weren't serious? Have a drink, Dad. The minister will take care of Prabal Kumar and our problems will be over. Hell, Dad, Sevak Chand must be serious. He didn't mention Mahatma Gandhi to Sharmaji even once in his last order."

Chris and Ajay Vir roared with laughter.

Ram Avtar continued to brood. "No," he finally said regretfully. "He may well be serious about protecting us and the factory, but he didn't even mention Prabal Kumar. And most of all," he said reflectively, "he said nothing at all about helping us end the strike."

Ajai Vir sat down too and digested this. "But Dad," he remonstrated, "the whole press was there at the factory. When the papers appear tomorrow and everyone sees what a thug Prabal Kumar is, he'll be finished. Kaput."

His father said nothing.

That same evening, surprisingly, Doordarshan carried the story of the attack on the workers though it didn't carry any pictures. This was hailed as a sign of openness in television since the episode reflected very poorly on the Government.

The next morning's newspapers prominently displayed the attack, all with pictures, some on the front page. One photograph later won an award. It showed Prabal Kumar standing silhouetted, eyes in the distance, on the car, bodies falling around him under the raised sticks and rods of his men, and in the background, a line of policemen watching from behind their shields.

Over the next few days, Ajai Vir read with disbelief that more and more company workers around Delhi were seeking to get Prabal to head their unions. The old leaders were being dumped like spoiled vegetables and virtually the entire industrial belt of Faridabad was turning to Prabal, the workers pleading with him to lead them. Overnight, he had become the leading trade union leader of Delhi. As a worker who was interviewed put it; "If a leader can do what Prabal sahib did and the power of the Government standing a few yards away could not dare to interfere, then which son of a businessman will dare to say 'No' to him? Nobody has that courage."

Political parties began to compete with each other in inviting him to be associated with them. They had found their labour wings decimated within a day and it made sense to bring in this man, so young, so successful and now with an army of votes at his command. However, Prabal Kumar made it clear that he planned to stay independent.

"I have no ambitions of becoming a political leader," he informed a business newspaper. "I am only interested in serving the toiling worker whose labour creates wealth for the proprietor and the country, but who is himself denied a fair share of the fruits of his toil. When I think of this injustice, I tell you," he told the reporter, "my blood boils and I cannot sleep. Until this evil is removed, I will work to the last breath in me. I only live," he had concluded, "to make life better for that poor man whose toil makes life better for us. This is my only interest in life. That is why I have never married, have no friends and have broken all links with my family. The workers are my only family and their happiness is my only wealth. I seek nothing for myself."

Ajai Vir read the interview. "Dad this is insane," he expostulated to his father, "the guy's a maniac and a killer. Do you think I should talk to my journalist friends?" He asked.

"For what?"

"Well, I could tell them what a loony this guy is. A couple of articles on that and it'll be all over for him. Everybody'll see through him. Dad, we could fight him with publicity."

Ram Avtar shook his head in impatience.

Shortly thereafter, one morning, there was a phone call for Ram Avtar. It was from an assistant to Prabal Kumar.

"You have had time now to study the list of demands by the workers of KapCo," he said. "I am hopeful that you are willing to accept them at once."

"If I accept them at once," said Ram Avtar, "then my factory will also have to close down at once. The demands total up to an additional wage bill of Rs. 10 crore per year. If we add that to the price of our product, our goods will be far more expensive than our competitors. We'll be driven out of business. Bankrupt. We will have to close down."

"That of course only you can decide," said the assistant. "But if you cannot afford to pay your workers, you should not have come into business at all. But now that you are in business, no matter what happens, the workers must be paid what are their rightful dues."

Ram Avtar recognised the beginning of a negotiation when he saw one. He sighed. "Let us meet," he said "and discuss."

But he was wrong. Backed by his lawyers, when he met Prabal Kumar's men, they talked every day for three days and found Prabal Kumar's people weren't interested in negotiating. Prabal wanted every single demand conceded exactly as listed, including taxi fare for the workers for the fifty yard distance from the highway where the public buses stopped, to the factory gate.

"All right," Ram Avtar had tried to compromise. "We'll

provide company buses so that they don't have to walk the fifty yards."

No, said the union men, they wanted the money, not the company transport.

"In any case," reasoned Ram Avtar, "the money you're asking for is far too much for that distance. Even a taxi would only charge five rupees since its well within the minimum distance and the workers could split that on the basis of the legally permissible five men per taxi. It would come to Re. 1 per worker. I would be happy to pay that. Including the ride back to the highway after work," he threw in generously.

No, said the union, nothing but the best for their members. They wanted air-conditioned and imported taxis for them for the journey.

"All right," tried Ram Avtar, "divided by five workers per air-conditioned and imported taxi, how much would it work out to?"

No, declined the union again. They wanted their men to travel in style. One worker per air-conditioned and imported taxi.

Ram Avtar sighed once more. "Give me a figure," he asked. "Its only fifty yards. How much would the air-conditioned and imported taxis charge?"

Not so easy to compute, explained the union. You see, they wanted that the workers should have the right to make side trips on the way from the highway to the factory.

"Where to?" asked Ram Avtar in amazement.

As far as the bar beside Badhkal Lake, responded the union, with the proviso, naturally, that the taxi could be further taken to the nearest open bar in case the Badhkal Bar was closed, had run out of stocks, or been afflicted by some other calamity.

"Then why not till Bangalore?" demanded Ram Avtar irately. "They never run out of beer."

Because, replied the union, hurt, we are not unreasonable men.

"I'm telling you Dad," swore Ajai Vir with conviction after this little episode, "the guy's loony tunes. Just plain loony tunes."

"No," disagreed Ram Avtar, "he knows exactly what he is doing. We were the example he made to those workers who defied him and we are the example he's going to make of what he can get for workers. Or if that fails, of what he can do to companies that don't bow down before him."

"What do we do then?" worried Ajai Vir. "We're dead if the strike carries on for too long and we're dead if we give in to these ridiculous demands. And he shows no signs of compromising. And of course the workers are far too petrified to think of breaking away from him again. What do we do?" he asked in anguish.

"We'll just," said Ram Avtar, "have to talk to him directly."

7

A week later, he woke up earlier than usual and getting out of bed, sat in front of his wife's photograph.

"It looks like no one can help us," he said aloud, as he sometimes did in times of great difficulty, to her. It made him feel as though she was actually there. "We're near the breaking point. Our goods are out of the market, our competitors are fast replacing us and day before yesterday morning our main banker refused to let us postpone the repayment of either the interest or the capital that we borrowed from them. Its outrageous. They know the circumstances, they know its beyond our control, they know the company has no income. How do they expect me to find the money to repay them? Its not that I want to default, its just that there is a strike on. Everyone knows that. What do I do? I wish you were here. I know there is nothing you could have done, but everybody needs somebody in his times of need. But today we'll know what Prabal Kumar wants."

He tinkled the little bell inviting the attention of the Gods and fell into an intense prayer.

An hour after his main banker had called him to say that his request for a postponement of KapCo's financial obligations had been denied and the bank was preparing legal steps to attach his property in case of default, he had telephoned Prabal Kumar. They had agreed to meet today and Ram Avtar felt he needed all the divine help he could muster on this crucial day.

Bending over in supplication one last time, he got up,

left the room and went in his Mercedes to the bus stop opposite the Dhaula Kuan Club.

There, as instructed, he waited for the bus going to Jaipur, got into it, bought a ticket from the conductor and sat silent, immersed in his fears, as they drove through Delhi, into Haryana and then crossed into Rajasthan.

The scenery changed from the green of the fields, to the brown and gold of Rajasthan. It was a remarkably sudden transformation, but Ram Avtar was in no mood to marvel at the wonders of nature. About ten minutes after they had entered Rajasthan, the driver, as though previously instructed, stopped the bus. Ram Avtar got down and another passenger disembarked with him. The bus drove off and the other man looked carefully up and down the road. No other vehicle or person was visible and with a gesture to Ram Avtar he plunged into the field beside the road. Almost immediately, they came to a small canal watering the field and followed that. After five minutes he stopped and carefully frisked Ram Avtar in case he was carrying a weapon or a recording device.

Satisfied, he resumed walking and after five minutes they saw a pump house, alongside which stood a blue Maruti which had obviously come down a mud path that could be seen going in the opposite direction. The man gestured towards the car and waited. Ram Avtar walked towards it, the door opened and Prabal Kumar stepped out of the driver's side.

Ram Avtar reached the car and they looked at each other over the roof. Prabal Kumar spoke a few sentences quietly. As Ram Avtar tried to answer him, he raised his hand sharply. Saying a few more sentences, he sat down in the Maruti, shut the door and drove away.

Tiredly Ram Avtar walked back to where his guide still waited and trudged back, each step more leaden than the last, till they reached the highway again. A green Matador van stood there and he got in and sat down. He looked around for his guide, but he had disappeared.

The van driver was a friendly sort and curious at being hired to wait in the middle of a highway. He was even more startled at the sudden appearance of this sahib with mud caked shoes. He tried to subtly get some answers from him, but the sahib didn't so much as acknowledge his questions. Eventually he gave up, resigned to leaving another mystery in life unresolved. Besides, the sahib was looking so bad tempered, that he wouldn't have been much of a conversationalist. And anyway he had been paid in advance by the man who had hired him. He always made sure of these things.

They entered the blaze of lights marking the suburbs of Delhi and as they reached the city itself, his passenger spoke his first and last words to him. "Stop here," he said, gesturing to a taxi stand. The van driver obliged. Ram Avtar got off and the van driver drove off, marvelling at the taciturnity of sahibs when there were so many interesting things in life to talk about.

Ram Avtar walked into the living room where Chris and Ajai Vir awaited him anxiously. When Ajai Vir had heard of the proposed meeting and the precautions to be followed he had immediately been full of ideas involving private detectives, stealthy shadowing and bugging devices. Ram Avtar had not humoured him. "I'll do as Prabal Kumar says," he had snapped. "Then lets see."

Now the boys were all agog. Wearily he seated himself and Ajai Vir rushed off to get him a drink even before a servant arrived. He returned while Jingle Bells was still tinkling in the air and handed the glass to his father.

"Well Dad?" he asked anxiously.

"He wants that we announce the immediate and total acceptance of all the demands totalling Rs. Ten crore per annum to the workers and he'll call off the strike the same day. And the workers will resume duties from that day itself."

"Big deal," said Chris and Ajai Vir simultaneously.

Ram Avtar waved at them to be quiet. "The first three months we pay the workers exactly as per the demands we have accepted and after that we pay them less the next month pleading the setback the strike has caused. The next month we pay even less and so on, till in the seventh month we go back to paying them just what we were paying them before the strike."

"And the workers will swallow that?" sneered Ajai Vir.

"Prabal Kumar guarantees it. He also guarantees that there will be no further work stoppages of any sort, or any labour trouble of any kind whatsoever for a period of ten years."

"Jeez," said Chris in bewilderment, "then what was the whole big deal about? The workers get nothing really and what in hell does he get out of it?"

"Fifteen crore rupees."

"Say what?" pleaded Chris.

"From us," explained Ram Avtar. "Those are his terms."

"How much is that in dollars?"

"Five million."

"No shit."

They all thought about it.

"Can we pay that kind of money Dad?" asked Ajai Vir.

Ram Avtar shook his head. "Not that much. Its completely unreasonable."

"Maybe I could negotiate with him Dad. I did a course on Negotiating in Business School."

"He's not going to meet us again. We just call to say yes or no. I presume if we say 'yes' then he'll tell us how we can meet again and instruct us on the ways of transferring the money."

"And if we say 'No?' "

"He didn't say, but I assume the strike continues, we're bankrupted, the other industrialists terrified into coughing up even more money and he appears as the hero of the workers. Any way you look at it, we lose. Any way you look at it, he wins."

"Jeez," marvelled Chris, "what a greaseball."

"We're worse off than when you met him Dad," complained Ajai Vir. "What do we do now?"

"I'm baffled," admitted Ram Avtar. "Liberalisation is in full swing. The Government is actively seeking foreign investments. Yet they're allowing the strike to continue, they are letting this union leader get out of hand. Who will want to invest in Delhi if they feel they will have their necks in the hands of Prabal Kumar who will make them pay wages that will make their products uncompetitive? It will finish the main advantage India has in attracting capital. It makes no sense to me at all."

"They're fools," expostulated Ajai Vir. "All politicians are fools. Crooks and criminals and idiots who'll ruin this country."

"Crooks and criminals, yes," agreed Ram Avtar, "idiots, no. And they're certainly not so idiotic as to ruin the country that's making them so rich. Not even a fool," reasoned Ram Avtar, talking more to himself than to the boys, "would kill his only cow. No," he said shaking his head decidedly, "the politicians are no fools."

"Then what Dad?" asked Ajai Vir at a complete loss. "What's happening?"

Ram Avtar looked into his glass for a long time as though it was a crystal ball hiding secrets. "Something," he said finally, "something's happening. And we have to find out what."

"Right," said Chris springing to his feet, "lets go and find out."

Ram Avtar smiled indulgently. "Saturday," he promised. "Saturday night we'll find out what's happening."

He got up and deep in thought, went to his room.

"Saturday?" queried Chris, "whats so special about Saturday for Christ's sake? What does he do on Saturday nights?"

Ajai Vir shrugged. "Goes a lot to the Gymkhana Club, that's all."

"What happens there on Saturday nights?"

"They serve great Scotch and terrible music."

"So, is it worth going to or what?"

"If you like watching people dance, not one of whom can keep time with the music. I'm telling you Chris, until you've seen a Joint Secretary Finance, responsible for our foreign exchange reserves, trying to do the twist in time to 'Strangers in the night', you don't know the meaning of real fear."

"Jeez, I guess so," said Chris dubiously, not sure, fortunately, what Joint Secretaries to the Government of India doing what they sincerely believed to be the twist, looked like. "But how's he going to find out what's up at this gymnasium?"

"Gymkhana," corrected Ajai Vir.

"Whatever."

"I suppose he has a friend or something who goes there. Its a favourite with bureaucrats. They may not do much work, but they do know what's going on in the Government."

"Well," grumbled Chris, "I guess we'll just have to wait."

Moodily he walked back to his room. The phone rang. "Sir," said Mr. Sunder, "Madam Kalpana called and left a message. She said she was phoning back because you had called her."

Chris's heart leapt. He couldn't remember if he had called her, but he wasn't about to complain. "I'll phone her right away," he enthused. "And how about you, old buddy?" he enquired, still in high spirits. "How's life been treatin' you?"

Mr. Sunder had stayed strangely distant for a self appointed guru after the Playboy magazine fiasco.

"Tip top shape with your kind blessings sir," responded Mr. Sunder embarrassedly.

"Great. And don't think I've forgotten about the socially relevant magazine for your friends. I'm looking into it. One day, before you know it, bingo, there it'll be."

"I am sure my friends are possessing deep gratitudes," whispered Mr. Sunder in case anyone nearby overheard, "now please excuse, there is phone on other line."

"Sure buddy," boomed Chris in great humour, "Maybe its Hugh Hefner calling personally." He roared uproariously.

Humming to himself, he punched Kalpana's number. He got her new answering machine. 'Shit,' he cursed, 'while I've been jerkin around old Sunder, she's split. Well,' he calmed down, 'I'll try later.'

He tried every day, virtually every hour, but she was never home, even at night. Since Ajai Vir was closetted most of the time with his father and the lawyers, she obviously wasn't with him either.

'Has she got another guy?' he wondered jealously. 'I'll kill him.' He reasoned that even if she had she would have been home sometime. 'Naah,' he thought, 'must have gone out of Delhi.' He wandered whether to ask Ajai Vir but decided it would look odd.

Saturday evening arrived and Ram Avtar left for what Chris kept referring to as the Gymnasium. They were sitting in Ajai Vir's room watching television and drinking while they waited for Ram Avtar to return. The blackboard with the three B's had been wiped clean since, explained Ajai Vir, there was no business to run at the moment. They did not speak much — Ajai Vir because he was tense and worried, Chris because he was trying to figure out where Kalpana might be. Dinner was wheeled in on a trolley by a servant but they barely touched it.

It was nearing midnight when a servant opened the door. "Sahib has asked you to come to the living room," he announced.

They walked down the hall and heard from a distance, after what seemed such a long time, Ram Avtar's fabled laugh. He was giving vent to his friendly, encouraging version. Somebody was being urged to talk. They quickened their steps and opened the door.

On the sofa, a drink in his hand, flushed but completely in control of himself, sat Ram Avtar, his laugh now a roguish one. Obviously they had interrupted a men's only joke. Next to him, they saw with shock, his head lolling, the mouth slurring, sprawled Sharmaji.

"Come in boys, come in," welcomed Ram Avtar standing up. "I bumped into Sharmaji by chance at the Club and

85

what a pleasant coincidence that he happened to be there. I requested and finally persuaded him to come to our humble little home because I told him how upset you both were at that scene at the Minister's office and how you both wanted to apologise to him."

Ram Avtar's finger's dug into Ajai Vir's arm like drills and he looked warningly at Chris.

"See Sharmaji," he said, "how thin both my boys have become after that day. They have been so upset that they have not taken any food for the last so many days. Ajai Vir keeps saying, 'How I could have said those horrible things about Sharmaji Uncle who is like a father to me.' And Chris said that a man as fine, upright and intelligent as Sharmaji should go to America where he would become an assistant to the President and a billionaire in no time at all. Isn't that so Chris?" he asked glaring.

"Damn right," corroborated Chris. "I said the first day I met you that what President Clinton really needs to get America out of the mess its in and going again is Sharmaji as his personal assistant. No doubt about that at all."

"I'm so sorry uncle," added Ajai Vir, his arm still aching from his father's fingers, "I just got so upset about that Prabal Kumar that I don't even know what I said."

"He," said Ram Avtar swooping up the baton instantly, "came home and cried, 'I don't care about KapCo,' he told me. 'But I have been rude to Sharmaji Uncle who is my senior and much more than my father could ever have been. He has always been my protector, adviser and refuge from storms ever since childhood," said Ram Avtar, magnificently over-looking the small fact that the two had met precisely twice in their lives. "Ajai Vir told me, 'I can never forgive myself' and locked himself in the bathroom where he cried for two days. Apologise again boys," demanded Ram Avtar.

"Sorry sir," the two mumbled like children.

Fortunately Sharmaji was too far gone to follow more than the bare gist of this incredible performance.

"Assistant to President Clinton?" he smirked cunningly at Chris.

"No question at all," assured Chris with all sincerity. "Greatest thing that could happen to the United States."

Sharmaji began to dribble with pleasure at what the prospect of being assistant to President Clinton would unfold.

"Not, of course," leapt in Ram Avtar, "that the Government of India would ever let Sharmaji leave. *Arre*, could a child survive without the sure and experienced hand of its mother? And the world knows that this is what Sharmaji is for whichever ministry is lucky enough to enjoy his presence. Boys, I must tell you in complete confidence, Sharmaji is not a man, he is a legend. An *avtar* of some hero from the *Panchatantra*."

It was Ajai Vir's turn to jab him in his back.

"I mean the *Mahabharta*, of course. Who would not know that?" hastily corrected Ram Avtar.

Sharmaji was oozing little bubbles of bliss.

"But tell me Sharmaji," Ram Avtar refilled the bureaucrat's sloshing glass with neat whisky. "When all India sings praises of your role in guiding the ministry correctly, when in the farthest and remotest corners of India the name Sharmaji is a coin with which you can purchase anything ..." he paused. That didn't sound right. "Anyway, where becoming another Sharmaji is the ambition of all little children and the name is the terror of every Government servant not to mention the dream of every Indian beauty. Ha ha ha," he leaned across and prodded Sharmaji's chest with a finger. "Don't think we have not heard of how Aishwarya Rai has publicly pursued Sharmaji across the length and breadth of the country and into the offices of the Government itself and made his life such a hell. Don't think we have not heard."

Of course he had heard no such thing and any self-respecting Indian beauty would have immolated herself rather than even acknowledge Sharmaji's existence, but Sharmaji had fallen into such a trance at the prospect of young but legendary beauties making his life a public hell, that Ram Avtar feared he may have died from an excess of joy.

"Yet Sharmaji," Ram Avtar returned skilfully to his theme, "despite your hand on our head, how can that bloody Prabal Kumar do this? Does he not know that we are Sharmaji's men?"

Sharmaji hiccuped, his hand waved feebly, "Above," he slurred "all above."

"Ah, the minister," understood Ram Avtar instantly. "But Prabal is a threat to Sevak Chand too. After consolidating his base among industrial workers, Prabal will move into Delhi and with the men and money on his side, he will not be stopped. Sevak Chand must know that. Prabal will wipe him out in Delhi, his own constituency."

Sharmaji was breathing shallowly. Ram Avtar shook him. "Why?" he asked, "why is Sevak Chand allowing it?"

Sharmaji belched. "*Ja*," he muttered.

"*Ja*?" puzzled Ram Avtar, "Go? You want to go somewhere? Home?

Sharmaji spoke again indistinctly. "Jha," he said.

Ram Avtar's eyes lit up. "Ah, yes, I see now."

"What? what?" demanded Ajai Vir.

"Jha is Sevak Chand's most bitter rival in Delhi politics. What Sharmaji has told us is that Prabal is being sup-
ported secretly by Jha. Obviously he hopes to make Prabal a
force able to topple Sevak Chand. Later he probably has
plans to make a deal with Prabal or knows a way to push
him out."

He turned again to Sharmaji. "But I don't understand.
Politics is one thing and this is just local Delhi politics. Its a
small matter. But liberalisation is a national economic policy.
The Prime Minister could flick Prabal Kumar out like a fly
from a cup of milk in an instant if he became an impediment
to that. The PM is the shrewdest of the lot, yet he's done
nothing. Why?"

Sharmaji tried to sit up but gave up the struggle and
subsided.

"Why?" insisted Ram Avtar urgently. This was now the
key. "Why is the PM not acting? Sharmaji," he shook his
shoulder roughly.

The bureaucrat's eye half opened and he tried to focus.
"CPM," he intoned thickly and collapsed. A snore emanated.

"He's a dead loss," said a disgusted Ajai Vir. "There is
no reason why the PM should let the CPM stop him from
removing Prabal. He doesn't need them right now."

"No, he's saying just the opposite," disagreed Ram Avtar.
"The PMO is using Prabal to get control of the unions before the CPM can. I had heard rumours that their cadres
were starting to become active in the Faridabad belt."

"Whats the CPM?" asked Chris.

"The Communist Party of India (Marxist)," explained
Ajai Vir. "They rule West Bengal."

"And Delhi industry would be a rich prize because if
the CPM unions can dominate it, they could create untold

problems and embarrassments for whichever party is in power, by organising strikes, processions and riots at the moments likely to earn them the greatest publicity," Ram Avtar spoke rapidly. "So the Congress wants to let a hero rise who can squash the Communists and who they must have means of controlling, that we know nothing about. KapCo happened to be his launch pad and that was just our bad luck." Now the brain that had watched Delhi's politics for forty seven years was racing. "But Jha alone can't promote Prabal to this point. He must have got the green signal from more senior people in the Congress party. That means they are ready to let Sevak Chand fall and Prabal replace him. Sevak must know this, yet he does nothing. Why?"

Ram Avtar paced up and down, oblivious to Sharmaji snoring in the chair. "Boys," he finally admitted, "we only have half the answer. Get the servants to put Sharmaji in the spare bedroom and I'll talk to him tomorrow. Ajai Vir, call his house and tell them that he has been detained by the minister to conduct urgent negotiations with us and our foreign partners and these will carry on all night and they shouldn't worry."

Ajay Vir did as he was told and they all went to sleep.

They next morning when he came out, he found his father helping a wan Sharmaji in the throes of the mother of all hangovers, into a car to take him home.

"Sharmaji," Ram Avtar pleaded quietly, for once sincere, holding the bureaucrat's hand, "my life's work is finishing before my eyes. My child has no future. Sevak Chand is in even deeper trouble. Yet he does nothing to break the strike. He gave you no instructions to force Prabal to a rational compromise, which you could easily do. I won't ask you why, since you can't obviously help me, but for the sake of my son, have pity on an old man who may not have much time left. Tell me, what can I do to get the minister's help?"

Sharmaji blinked painfully and tried to clear his furred tongue to say something as he edged painfully into the car. "Smile," he muttered thickly.

"Sir, what?" anxiously asked Ram Avtar, hanging onto the door, not sure he'd heard right.

"Make the minister smile," said Sharmaji clearly as the car pulled away.

8

Once again they were all seated in the living room.

"Make the minister smile?" questioned Ajai Vir. "Dad, Sharmaji obviously means money. The minister's a politician. Lets give him so much money that he won't just smile, he'll laugh like a hyena. It'll be cheap compared to Prabal Kumar."

"No," disagreed his father. "Sevak Chand has made so much money in his career that he could pay whatever Prabal wants from us and not even notice. Not of course," he acknowledged, "that he would have the slightest objection to making even more money. But now he's fighting for his very political survival. And yet he's not lifting a finger," he marvelled. "It could only be that there is pressure on him from above to not move."

"That could only be the PM," said Ajai Vir. "Sevak Chand wouldn't listen to anyone else. But Dad, if he realizes that Kumar will destroy him in a few years, would he listen even to the PM?"

It was a good question. Ram Avtar nodded in appreciation. "For a while," he said, "perhaps for quite a long while depending on the pressure the PM has put on him."

"And the PM would apply that kind of pressure to ensure that Prabal rises?"

"Definitely," said Ram Avtar. "Liberalisation is crucial for the Congress. We know that the CPM is dead against it. If they control Delhi's industrial unions, they can create havoc. Anything that happens in Delhi is transmitted worldwide. If the labour situation in the city is made to look uncertain by the CPM, then investors all over the globe will think its the same India-wide and therefore the country is not a good place to invest in. Imagine," he urged, "if every time there was a major business delegation from a foreign country and they found strikes and black flags greeting them, how do you think they would react? No," Ram Avtar concluded, "Prabal Kumar is a creation of the Congress to fight off the CPM. The problem is," he said more slowly, "that though most of the workers are flocking to him because of what he did at KapCo, they will leave him equally rapidly if he isn't able to deliver the goods. And since the focus is on KapCo, its us that he has to establish his reputation with. He wants to show that he has obtained such concessions for the workers that they are unmatched in the history of Indian industry."

"You mean he doesn't really want the five million dollars from us?" asked Chris.

"Yes he does. Because the way he's planned it, it'll make him appear to be the God of the workers and it will let him make his money too. Don't forget we are supposed to pay the workers as agreed for three months. He probably hopes that by then he will have got other businessmen to concede to his demands and we'll be forgotten."

"Then should we pay up?" asked Ajay Vir.

"We cannot," said his father shortly. "We are a small company and as you know not a very profitable one. Margins have been under pressure for a long time. And whatever I made, I mostly reinvested in the business. We simply do not have that kind of cash."

"What do we do then?" asked Chris.

"If even the PM is supporting Prabal," said Ajai Vir,

"then we're dead ducks. I mean there's nobody above. If they want to make an example out of us, if they want to show that Prabal is God's gift to workers because of what he can extract from KapCo, then what chance do we have? I mean the Congress Party rules India, for God's sake!"

"Does that mean its, like, finished?" Chris enquired.

"Yeah, those are some mean guys I tell you," said Ajai Vir bitterly. "You know Dad", it suddenly struck him, "I'll tell you what we could do. We could support the BJP in the next elections and when they beat the Congress, we could get to keep the factory going. Hell, I'll even campaign for them."

Ram Avtar didn't even bother to look irritated. But clearly the mind that had seen him through so many business battles was turning the situation around as though it was a Rubik's Cube, looking for that flash of insight that would make everything fall just right.

"There's just one thing I can think of," he finally said slowly. "Its a long shot and I'm not sure how much of the media speculation is correct, but there may be one person who could help us."

Both Ajai Vir and Chris sat forward. "Who?"

"Number 10."

"What?" asked a bewildered Chris.

"Number Ten, Janpath," explained Ram Avtar.

"Yeah," exulted Ajai Vir. "Mrs. Sonia Gandhi."

"Right," understood Chris. "That lady. But is she like, more powerful than the Prime Minister?"

"No, of course not," said Ram Avtar. "But she's one person who gets listened to by everyone in the Congress. If we could persuade her that this Congress strategy is suicidal

94

and against everything Rajiv stood for, she might speak to someone."

"And they'd have to listen to her!" exclaimed Ajai Vir in triumph.

"No they would not," said his father now clearly irritated. "But at least we'd get listened to if she spoke on our behalf. And a very powerful section in the Congress would certainly accept what she had to say."

"Great," said Chris getting up, "let's go talk to her."

Ram Avtar smiled wryly. "She doesn't meet anyone. And I don't know her at all. We have to find someone with approach. That's the Indian way."

"You know someone?" asked Ajai Vir expectantly.

"Not directly. But we'll have to ask around. Put out word that we are looking for a suitable person with approach. We will screen them carefully and for the right person cost would be no consideration."

"Yeah," gloated Ajai Vir, "and after Sonia speaks, the minister will have to smile."

So the word was rapidly spread among the armies of fixers and middlemen who throng Delhi and Lal Verma, who had returned from the hospital — in disgrace, it must be said, but who had been accepted back anyway — did the initial screening.

The final interviews were held at the Punjabi Bagh residence in the living room by Ram Avtar personally, with Ajai Vir and Chris sitting in.

The first applicant didn't last very long.

"How do you know the family?" asked Ram Avtar, the moment the man had seated himself.

Lal Verma, who was bringing the candidates in, explained.

"He has a long connection sir. He has known them since long. Please speak," he urged the man.

"Myself was doll repairer of Priyankaji," explained the first candidate. "Due to quality of work, I am in good books for long."

Ram Avtar surveyed him closely. Clad in kurta pyjamas, fat, with his lips stained with *paan*, he was not a pretty sight. Aware of Ram Avtar's close appraisal, the man decided to further his chances.

"I am often saying to Indiraji," he said casually, but stopped significantly to remove a piece of *paan* from his lips and flick it away, "Madam, I am often saying, Priya *bitiya* is like my own ..." he faltered as Ram Avtar vigorously rang the bell that had been placed beside him for just such an occasion.

The servant standing at the door stepped in instantly.

"Please take this gentleman outside," Ram Avtar instructed. "Ask the next candidate to come in please," he told Lal Verma.

"What's wrong Dad?" asked Ajai Vir, as the man left bewildered. "He does seem to have known them a long time. If he repaired Priyanka's dolls, at least we should listen to him," he urged.

"Yeah," agreed Chris, "kids always remember people like that."

"He's lying," grunted Ram Avtar. "Anybody who had referred to Indiraji's grand-daughter as 'Priya *bitiya*' in her presence wouldn't have lived fifteen minutes, much less till now. Next," he called.

The gentleman who entered looked athletic. Tall, fit, dressed in a brown safari suit, he had a pleasant open face with a somewhat fixed smile, a crew cut and a gracious manner.

He did a reverential *namaste* to everybody present and sat down.

Lal Verma announced his credentials. "Mr. Chowdhary is the Secretary General of the Indo-Global Friendship Society which has many well known former ministers and ex-M.Ps on its Board of Governors."

"What does your society do, Mr. Chowdhary?" asked Ram Avtar.

Mr. Chowdhary smiled even more broadly. "We encourage friendship between India and all the countries of the world," he explained. "Unlike many of the other societies," his tone became somewhat disparaging as his smile turned into a sneer, "that only look at friendship between India and only one other country, we look at all the countries. You understand, I hope?" he enquired.

Ram Avtar understood perfectly. Why restrict yourself to freebies from one country, when you could get them from all countries.

"So," resumed Mr. Chowdhary, his smile broadening again, assuming that his interviewer's silence indicated he was impressed," I have taken as our motto the old Sanskrit saying: 'The world is one.' " He raised one finger to indicate 'one', but Ram Avtar raised his whole hand.

"How," he asked peremptorily, "do you know them?"

Mr. Chowdhary was unmoved by such rudeness. "Rajivji had a special soft corner for me," he revealed modestly.

"Why?"

"You see, due to my belief that the world is one which I have accepted from my childhood days, I decided that in order to promote the concept of universal brotherhood among all the countries, I would drive on a tricycle through all countries of the world. I knew that Rajivji with his broad vision,

97

noble ideas and global temperament, would support me fully in this. Therefore, through a close relative of mine who was personally known to him, I sent a personal letter inviting him to take a little time off from his onerous duties as Prime Minister for this great cause and as an inspiration to all the world, to sit behind me on the tricycle through Pakistan and Afganistan at least until Iran. My letter was put up to him and in his own handwriting he has written," Mr. Chowdhary paused here to ensure that his audience grasped the significance, "he has written, 'This guy's nuts.' " He stopped and his vacuous smile threatened to extend a full inch beyond his face. "I was so moved and inspired by his encouraging sentiments that I decided to go twice around the world. Here is the letter with his noting," he said, producing the letter, "unfortunately before I could tricycle very far," his smile turned down into sorrow, "my father suffered from certain heart problems due to sadness at my leaving and on account of family pressures I had to return from the Minto Bridge itself. But I wrote to Rajivji again placing my services at his disposal since we were on the same wave length. My close relative told me that due to work pressures he was not able to reply immediately and ..."

Ram Avtar rang the bell violently again. When Mr. Chowdhary exited, he asked Lal Verma, "Is this the best you can do?"

Verma looked apologetic. "Sir, Soniaji meets very few people and the selected people she does meet would never agree to mention our problem to her. We have to make do with whatever we can. I am doing my best."

Ram Avtar sighed in understanding. "Soniaji's temperament is well known," he agreed. "Send in the next."

He brightened at the next individual. This was a *sadhu* dressed in saffron, with twinkling eyes and a long white beard.

"Sit down, sit down," said the *sadhu* blessing them all with his hand, though no one had shown any signs of standing up.

"I have renounced all worldly matters," he announced, seating himself. "I have a small *ashram* above Hardwar where I have settled. I never come to the city, but of course the great people of the city are always troubling me," he laughed gently. "But when news of your plight reached me, I was so moved that I felt I would be failing in my obligation as a person learned in the *Vedas* if I did not use my powers at this time. After all, it is said in the *Shastras*, 'True knowledge comes with difficulty,' " he smiled beatifically. "But I ask nothing for myself. I have no wants and my few needs are looked after by my devotees. But for the sake of maintaining the *ashram* and for my disciples who are all like my children, all donations are welcome. It is not an income tax exempt trust because I accept donations only in our Swiss bank account since the conversion rate there is more favourable. Of course, if the Rupee keeps strengthening we may need to apply for tax exempt status here but that is not the case currently. However, it should not be a problem for a big industrialist like you. We all understand the need for a foreign account for a big man like you, otherwise how would the proceeds from under-invoicing and over-invoicing of exports be channelised safely?" He laughed gently at the foolish ways of the world and resumed before his nonplussed listeners. "Of course I do not need to discuss the exact amounts I expect before a reputed tycoon like yourself, but you would understand that the expenses of an *ashram* are always increasing so a percentage of the amount saved due to my humble efforts should be fixed and fifty percent of that deposited in advance naturally. Naturally there is no question of mistrust," he laughed gently again, his eyes twinkling even more merrily, "but the world has become so materialistic. And I know that it goes without saying to an experienced and eminent industrialist such as you, that in the event of the Swiss franc falling against the Rupee, you would have to compensate at a rate acceptable which would be that of the franc to the Rupee today. But I happen to know this rate because one of my devotees ..."

Ram Avtar interrupted with folded hands. "Swamiji," he pleaded "how do we know the work will be done?"

Swamiji's eyes clouded with pain at this mistrust. He dug into the robe of his saffron gown and produced an object. "My visiting card," he offered.

Ram Avtar read it. "Swamiji Ahimsa Sagar Dosco Walle," he pronounced. "Retired Chief Clerk, Doon School."

He looked with sudden interest at the Swami.

"Ah," he said.

The Swami smiled even more benignly and blessed them all again.

"Swamiji, when did you work at Doon?" Ram Avtar asked.

Swamiji's eyes twinkled eloquently. "At the right time of course," he assured them.

Ram Avtar was not so easily taken in. "How did you come to know Rajivji?" he enquired. "After all there must have been many clerks at Doon?"

Swamiji graciously acknowledged such terrestrial suspicions. "In those days, before I abandoned worldly pursuits, when Rajivji was studying, I was incharge of the tuck shop," he revealed. "And Rajivji," he added significantly, "was a healthy young man."

"But why would Rajivji have remembered somebody handing over his sweets to him?" asked Ram Avtar, ever the hard headed businessman.

Swamiji was unfazed. "Even then my spiritual powers were manifest," he confessed with smiling humility. "Somehow I sensed a radiance in the child, a feeling of destiny. I don't know how to explain it."

"Perhaps the fact that he was the Prime Minister's grandson might have had something to do with it," suggested Ajai Vir tartly.

The look Swamiji shot him was not benign. "I decided in my own humble way to encourage the little one however I could. So whenever it was his turn for tuck, I always slipped him an extra sweet, or a biscuit above the quota. It was so little for one so glorious," he laughed deprecatingly.

"Any proof?" demanded Ram Avtar.

Swamiji dug out an old black and white photograph, obviously much thumbed. It was Swamiji all right, minus the robe and the beard, handing a biscuit packet to a youthful Rajiv Gandhi in his school uniform.

"Rajivji," pointed out Swamiji looking with smiling though snide triumph at Ajai Vir, "looks grateful."

"Yes," conceded Ram Avtar, reluctantly impressed. "Swamiji," he concluded decisively, "Please leave your local phone number and address with my secretary. We will revert to you by today evening."

Swamiji swept to his feet, a regal yet saintly figure. "50%," he intoned blessing them, "advance deposit of 50%," he murmured, sailing away, "Swiss bank only," his voice trailed off.

101

"How many more?" Ram Avtar asked Lal Verma.

"Just two sir."

"Well, send in the next. And Verma, call up your contact in the Congress Party and find out how Soniaji is disposed towards the Swami. I think we may have found our man. The family will not be able to resist someone who was such a touching part of Rajivji's past."

The new man was short, simply dressed, and businesslike.

Ram Avtar asked him, "You represent a friendship society?"

The man looked offended. "Far more than that. I am Mathur of the India-Italian Brother cum Sister Group. Naturally it is registered. You can well understand my influence. What service can I do?"

"What exactly does your group do?"

"We are a group of Indian men who have been so impressed by the lady like virtues of Italian ladies, that each one has adopted at least one Italian lady as his *rakhi* sister. My own *rakhi* sister, naturally is Soniaji."

"I see," pondered Ram Avtar. "And when did your group discover the sisterly virtues of Italian ladies?"

"Shortly after Rajivji became PM, but that was only," Mr. Mathur's voice rose sharply, "because we had not been aware of Italian ladies before that. If we had, we would assuredly have formed our group much earlier."

"Naturally," agreed Ram Avtar, "Are there any Italian men by chance in your group who have adopted Indian women as their *rakhi* sisters?"

"All efforts are on in this direction," crisply assured Mathur. "But we find that Italian men do not possess very brotherly feelings towards ladies of any nationality whatsoever. It is proving a bitter disappointment."

102

"I can understand," sympathised Ram Avtar, still cautious in case there was something to the man. "I assume you send *rakhis* to all the sisters?"

Mathur nodded. "Of course," he said curtly.

"Well, who are the other sisters?"

"Sophia Lauren and Claudia Cardinale."

"Very impressive. And do your *rakhi* sisters ever reply?"

"The sisters are too busy wearing the *rakhis* to write-shite," Mathur brushed aside the question impatiently. "But of course they appreciate the sentiments."

"How about you?" enquired Ram Avtar. "Don't the brothers ever write to the sisters?"

"Naturally," said Mathur in surprise. "What brother does not write to his sister?"

"Very true," applauded Ram Avtar, "but do the sisters, specifically your own *rakhi* sister, ever write back to you?"

Mathur looked remote and mysterious. A small smile played about his lips. "These are family matters," he explained. "I am not at liberty to discuss them with outsiders. But you can be assured that I am very free and frank in my own letters."

"As you should be," congratulated Ram Avtar warmly, his hand moving towards the bell.

Sensing the motion, Mathur broke into a sweat. "Of course," he added swiftly, "in my own case the relationship is even closer because I have myself descended from an Italian."

Ram Avtar's eyebrows rose as his hand paused over the bell. He waited.

"You see," quickly resumed Mathur. Chris could smell the sweat coming off him. "My name Mathur is an Indianisation of the Italian original. It is actually Mat-Hur. And I am the

103

last in the direct line after many centuries of travels, of the original Italian who you may have heard of and about whom Hollywood made a film. The famous Ben-Hur. Hence my name, Mat-Hur. Soniaji herself ..."

The bell shrieked in horror and Mr. Mathur was flung out.

The last candidate didn't look too prepossessing either. He was young, slim, but didn't look like he had the confidence or experience to handle such a delicate matter.

"Who is he?" asked Ram Avtar.

"Mr. Mehfooz was a caddy at the Army Golf Club sir," informed Verma.

"Rajiv never played golf." said Ram Avtar decisively, reaching for the bell.

Verma added swiftly, "Now sir, he is a marker at the Rashtrapati Bhawan tennis courts."

"Oh?" asked Ram Avtar, unimpressed.

"Rahul goes there to play tennis sir."

Ram Avtar's hand moved back. "Mehfooz bhai," he enquired, "you must be meeting the young man frequently?"

Mehfooz nodded embarrassedly. "He's a good boy sir. Very friendly and unassuming."

"How many markers are there at the courts?"

"The *ustad* and three of us."

"And Rahul recognises you?"

"Yes sir," he nodded.

"And the work has been explained to you. Do you think you can do it?"

"Yes sir, I will ask the other markers to also talk. And of course Rahulji listens a lot to the *ustad*."

"On all matters, or only in tennis?"

"So far only in tennis sir, but we'll try this too."

"Well at least you're honest," acknowledged Ram Avtar. "Does Rahul have a high regard for you as a coach?"

"Yes sir."

"Why?"

"I improved his back hand sir."

Ram Avtar felt a stir of excitement. "Permanently?"

"Yes sir. He was slicing too much. I made him change his grip and hit through the ball."

"And Rahul?" Ram Avtar was gripping his chair. "What did he say?"

"He said I had made a new player out of him sir."

Lal Verma interjected. "Very significant statement sir. It suggests a deep gratitude that wants a way to express itself."

"Perhaps," said Ram Avtar, considering. "Okay Mehfoozji, we will contact you if necessary."

The lad left.

"The Swami's our best bet," opined Ajai Vir.

"Yup," agreed Chris, "shrewd guy."

"Regrettably sir, there are problems with him," interrupted Verma.

"If its the money," said Ram Avtar, "we'll bargain him down."

"No sir, its worse. As you suggested, I contacted my friend in the Congress while you were talking to the other candidates to enquire about Swamiji's status at 10, Janpath. I'm sorry sir, my information is that Soniaji appreciates that he knew Rajivji from his school days, but blames Swamiji for Rajivji's tooth cavities. After all, he provided the extra biscuits and sweets. She doesn't want him passing these on to the children too. He's *persona non grata*."

Ram Avtar looked bitter.

"Then its the tennis marker," he said, "but there's not much hope."

And so it proved to be. Eventually, the marker, his colleagues and their *ustad*, failed to muster the courage to even broach the subject, in whatever garbled fashion, to young Rahul and so that attempt failed, still born.

9

Chris sat moodily in the bar at the Oberoi Hotel. For once he was able to stretch out his legs luxuriously in front and he had become a frequent visitor, thinking fondly of it as the only bar in Delhi built with football players in mind.

The discreet colours and hushed service should have soothed him but he was depressed. He had eaten at their continental restaurant alone and now he was sitting by himself, staring down at the blue of the swimming pool, glowing softly under the lights.

'Poor guys,' he thought. 'What a mess. And just no way out for them. Nothing I can do either. Jeez,' he thought, 'just as you begin to really like this country, something happens to scare you off. Who in hell knows in America that the guys here could be so cunning and so ruthless. Shit, the rest of the world thinks Indian politicians are all like Gandhi, sitting around in bedsheets and doing that meditation and stuff and look at the kind of things they're upto. Wreck a business a guy's built up over his whole life just because they've got some plan. Real neat.'

He stirred his drink. There had still been no sign of Kalpana. She had called once while he was out, but when he phoned her, he got the answering machine again. Obviously, she had come to town and then gone out again. 'At least she called,' he thought. 'There's still hope.' He thought some more. 'But hope for what? She was going to marry Ajai Vir. And if news got out and particularly now, shit,' he shuddered at the prospect. 'But man, what a woman,' he marvelled.

'If I hadn't been such a jerk, at least I'd have seen a lot more of her. But shit,' he thought disgustedly 'what the hell do you expect of a football player. Can't talk shit. Spend all your life being hit all day from every angle, knock all the language out of anyone. Not that I got much chance to develop that,' he thought self-pityingly. 'I never needed to go to class and learn and stuff. The coach took care of all that. And all my friends are football players too and they're not much for talking. Hell,' he snorted sourly, 'you're lucky if they can grunt at the right moments when they're in bed.'

He signalled for another glass to the waiter and it was instantly brought over.

'But what the hell happens to the Kapoors now?' he wondered. He wasn't directly involved, but hell, they had become friends and what the hell were friends for? 'Jeez, I just wish there was something I could do. I like the guys, and boy, whats happening to them is bad, just real bad. But its all heavy political stuff that I don't even understand. If they want me to hit someone I can do that,' he thought with sudden savagery, 'that I've been taught to do real good.'

He thought with pleasure of making a tackle on the slender figure of Prabal Kumar. 'So you like getting guys bashed with rods, do you?' he'd say to him as he flew forward, launching himself like a battering ram, knocking the guy flat. 'So, I'd say,' fantasised Chris viciously 'you like hurting people, do ya?' He'd hold Kumar's hair with one hand and with the other his fist would land full blows, with the entire weight of his body behind them, on Prabal Kumar's face. 'Well,' thought Chris with pleasure, 'I'd say 'how d'you like that yourself? I don't need no iron rods, you notice?' I'd say, 'how'm doing with just these?' And with every heavy punch more of Prabal's bones would break, first of course the nose.

Blood would smear itself everywhere and the flesh would raise and get pulpy. Prabal Kumar would be screaming through his broken teeth and bleeding mouth, but Chris would keep working him over. Then, ..."

"Actually", said a distinguished - sounding though neutral voice just behind him, "you can help."

For a moment it didn't register with Chris.

The voice repeated, as though it had read his mind. "That's what friends are for."

Chris struggled to turn around and look. But the Oberoi bar's chairs are meant to sink lower into, not to turn around in. Before he could complete the manoeuvre, the man patted him gently on the back and came and stood in front of Chris. "The point is," he asked, "do you really want to help?"

"Sure," said Chris, dazed, still struggling. He stopped and looked at the man. "But who the hell are you?"

The man smiled. "All in good time," he assured.

He had nice teeth, thought Chris, now sizing him up. Small moustache, medium height, looked fit, wearing tinted glasses, relaxed but alert, wouldn't stand out anywhere, but he appeared to be highly trained, though at what Chris couldn't figure out. He seemed unobtrusive, but aware.

'Who is this guy?' thought Chris. "So what d'you want?" he demanded, suddenly belligerent, rising unsteadily to his full towering height. "If this is some sort of a pick up buddy, you're going to get more than you ever believed possible."

The man smiled again and made a soothing gesture. "I just wanted to know how far you're willing to go to help the Kapoors, that's all," he said. "Well? How much of a friend are you? Are you willing to let them get finished?" he demanded.

"Hey, no way," protested Chris immediately. "We're

buddies. I'd do anything to help," he said, a bit drunk, "anything. But," he raised a threatening finger, "I ain't going to bed with no guy for that, you savvy?"

The man smiled again. "No one would ask that. But you are ready to help," he said more to himself than to Chris. "Very well, may we discuss this further in my room upstairs? Follow me," he ordered.

Chris hesitated, then went after him. "Okay," he said, catching up with the man he looked down at him narrowly, "just remember what I said," he threatened. "OK? No bed scenes."

The man didn't answer.

They went up in the elevator to the fourth floor and walked down the corridor. He produced a set of keys, opened a door and they walked in. The lights were on. The door closed and the man gestured for Chris to sit at a small round table near the window. A normal sized chair stood on one side and a large armchair on the other. Relieved, Chris hastily seated himself in the comfortable armchair which was just right for his size. A full glass waited in front of him.

The man gestured to it. "Kentucky bourbon," he offered.

Chris was startled. "My favourite." It was both a question and an exclamation. He took a long draught and sighed with pleasure.

The man said nothing.

"Okay," Chris put down the glass. "Business time. Talk turkey. Who are you and how do I get the Kapoors out of this jam?"

The man stared at him intently for a while. "Lets just say I represent some people who have an interest in this part of the world. And your job is very simple. You have to find out if the Kapoors are willing to go into another line of business."

110

"Why the hell should they?" demanded Chris belligerently. "The old man's spent a lifetime in it and no union prick is going to kick him out. I'll bust his ass for sure. And anyway," he concluded, "the old man don't know no other business."

The man let a silence develop that seemed full of menace. "It is not for you to enquire why something is to be done," he said staring intently at Chris, "just do as told. You," he cut short as Chris began to object in outrage, "will be very well paid for it."

This quietened Chris. He thought for a moment. "How well paid?" he asked.

Something seemed to flash behind those shaded lenses. "The new business the Kapoors get into," he said, "you will get the franchise for all the goods needed, all the knowhow necessary to run the business will be provided to you. You will not have to lift a finger. You will become extremely rich in your own right. We'll do the running, you'll make the money."

"Yeah," excitement began to grow in Chris. But he fought it down.

"I ain't doing nothing against this country," he warned. "They're all right. Don't give a shit 'bout nobody, know what I mean. But they're okay."

Once again the man constructed a silence that spoke more eloquently and violently then anything he had said. "My instructions to you are for you to find out if the Kapoors are willing to enter any other line of business. I hope I will not have to repeat myself again?" he asked sharply.

"Oh, hey, no, Jeez, okay, hey, you're the boss. How much money will I make Stateside?"

"There will be a shop in every major city. Each will make a profit. All of it yours."

"Wow," Chris began to count the number of major cities. "Hey, why not the, you know, larger towns as well? Lot of dough there."

"In the second stage."

"Yup. Sounds good to me."

The man reached to a side table and handed a brown paper envelope to Chris.

"Five thousand rupees," he said, "for petty cash."

"All right," exulted Chris. We're in business." He stood up and held out his hand. "Lets shake pardner."

The man studied him once again and then briefly shook his hand. Chris was surprised at the strength in his grip.

"Just remember," the man's voice had turned freezing. There was a real menace to it. "No one must learn of this meeting. No one must know of our agreement." The voice rose. "Not Mr. Kapoor, not Ajai Vir, not Mr. Sunder, not Kalpana. Is that clear?" The voice cut like a lash across Chris's face.

He jumped "Hey, shit, all right," he protested, confused at how this man knew all his friends. "Jeez, I can keep a secret." He clutched the envelope.

"Just remember," reminded the man, "a chain of stores across America. All yours."

Chris began to smile again. "Yeah," he dreamed. "Hey pardner," he beamed, "no sweat. Mum's the word."

"I will call you soon," said the man.

"You want me to, like, call you here? I mean if I find out soon?" asked Chris.

"I will no longer be here." The man gestured at Chris to leave. "Now go."

Chris left. At the door he looked back. The man was sitting there impassively, his tinted glasses intent.

"Aah, how do I know it's you?" he asked. "Like, do you have a name?"

The man's lips thinned into a smile, both ironic and a sneer. "Aiyar", he said. "My name is Mian Shankar Aiyar."

Chris found himself in the corridor, his mind clouded. "Jeez," he groped, pressing the button for the elevator. "I'm sure I've heard that name somewhere."

There was a loud ring, a red light flashed and the elevator door opened. Chris stepped in and nodded to the other occupant, a short, fat man, apparently South American, sweating profusely and wearing a gaudy shirt. Chris could smell the reek of liquor on his breath.

One floor above the ground level, the elevator stopped. The fat man stepped out and looked suddenly at Chris. His face was wet, his mouth twitched and his eyes showed a terrible strain. The door shut.

Chris reached the lobby, went to the portico and one of the enormous doormen waved for a taxi for him. He got in, "Punjabi Bagh," he instructed the driver. He settled back for the long drive.

As the taxi reached the end of the driveway a van roared by, its horn blaring. 'Aiyar Cargo,' announced the sign on its side.

Chris began to think about the events of the night. 'I ain't doin' nothin' wrong,' he reassured himself. 'Maybe they should move into a new line of business.' The taxi stopped at a red light. The car in front had a message on its rear window. 'Aiyar & Co. Chartered Accountants.'

'Well,' thought Chris, 'what the hell could go wrong? They start a new business, get rich, I go back Stateside, get rich. Everybody's happy. Everybody scores a touch down.'

A truck thundered towards them, its headlights on full beam. All he could see was a large demon's face with it's tongue hanging out above the front windscreen and an illuminated sign that glowed 'Aiyar Dance Group.'

'Sure are a lot of Aiyars around,' thought Chris. 'Maybe that's why the guy's name sounds so familiar.'

Two motor cyclists came roaring down the road almost under the wheels of the taxi. The driver braked furiously as they flashed by. The pillion rider of the first was holding a banner with one hand, obviously meant to put up somewhere, which was held by the pillion rider of the second motor cycle.

It read, 'Aiyar Cloth House. Special sale.'

Despite the great offer he had just received Chris began to feel uneasy. He wondered why. As they passed a ground, deserted at this time of the night, Chris saw a row of large paintings of people who were obviously going to address a gathering there the next day. His taxi driver pointed to one of a cherubic smiling figure.

"Mani Shanker Aiyar," reported the driver, "famous M.P." He didn't say another word.

'This is ridiculous,' thought Chris. 'How can there be so many Aiyars in just one city? But then,' he reasoned, calming himself down, why shouldn't there be? Maybe its like Smith in England.'

His eye was caught by a hot air balloon tethered near the road, floating fifty feet in the air. 'Visit Trade Fair at Pragati Maidan', urged the banner wrapped around it. Below it were the words, "Space, courtesy Nutech Ball Bearings.'

'Thank God,' said Chris, 'I thought I was going nuts.'
He leaned back in relief.

Their car slowed as they passed some men intently repairing the road. 'Good guys,' thought Chris, 'they'll finish by the morning so it'll be opened for traffic before the rush hour. They're learning,' he thought with a chuckle, 'sometimes I nearly approve of this country.'

The taxi began to accelerate as they went by the work-gang so he just about glimpsed the sign, 'Aiyar Road Repairers.'

He began to feel queasy. By now they were approaching the Kapoor residence and when Chris saw the policemen guarding it, he began to feel much more relieved. The guard saluted. The gates opened and they drove in. Chris paid the driver and leapt out. Whatever demon it was pursuing him, if there was a demon, would have a tough time getting past Delhi's Armed Police.

He walked past the police gypsy that had stood there for the last few days in the driveway and waved at the dozing policemen who did not stir. He strode past, looking at the slumbering cops, stopped wondering if he had actually seen something and walked back to the parked car. A small panel alongside the hood had engraved on it, 'Aiyar Auto Works.'

He walked much more rapidly to his room, slammed the door and for the first time since moving in, locked it. Dazed and fearful, breathing harshly, he went to the bathroom and brushed his teeth. 'What the shit is going on?' he tried to think. He wet and soaked his face and as he was washing it off he saw on the mirror a few inches away from him, a thin label, 'Aiyar Mirrors.'

He leapt back in panic, 'How had that got there? It hadn't been there that morning. Or had it?' he examined it closely. It was starting to peel with age and there were flecks of rust along the edges. 'Must have been there all along,' he thought unsteadily, 'I'm going to pieces. Jesus, how much did I have to drink? Steady on boy,' he cautioned himself.

The light in the bathroom went off. 'Shit,' he thought. 'Great.' But the lights in the bedroom were on. 'A blown fuse,' he calmed himself. 'Christopher' he said to himself severely, 'you're becoming an old woman.'

He strolled back to the bedroom and the lights there went off too. The light in the bathroom came on.

Chris felt his hands begin to shake. Through the dim light he saw his water glass and jug and drank down two quick glasses. He picked up the intercom.

"Hello," said Mr. Sunder.

"Mr. Sunder," Chris' voice shook, " The lights in my room have gone."

"I am sending bulb right away sir."

The lights came back on.

"Mr. Sunder," his voice was going to pieces, "the lights have returned."

"Very fine sir. Must be due to voltage fluctuation. Cheap equipment is being dumped due to liberalisation sir."

Chris hung up and his eye fell on the afternoon newspaper that had been left for him. The headline blared at him. "Meenakshi to star in Aiyar film." There was an accompanying photograph of a young actress posing with a smiling old man with a long white beard.

Chris called again. His voice sounded ragged, "Mr. Sunder, are there a lot of Aiyars in Delhi?"

"Plenty sir," said Mr. Sunder, disguising his astonishment at the question at this time of the night. If Mr. Kapoor's guests wanted to discuss the ethnic distribution of India's population, it was his duty to respond. "Many more in Madras of course sir," he added helpfully. "If you're wishing to meet some ..."

"Meet some," grated Chris, "there are too many already around me." He banged down the phone on a stupefied Mr. Sunder.

He strode to the cupboard and dragged out his suitcase, deciding desperately to somehow get out of there. The yellowing newspaper lining the bottom of the case had a discreet story that somehow attracted his eye. 'Aiyars not eligible for reservation quota says High Court,' it read.

With a cry, Chris flung away the suitcase, unbolted the door and raced to the office area. He threw open the door and stood there panting and heaving. "Mr. Sunder," he gasped to that startled worthy, wide-eyed at this apparition, "call the police. The Aiyars are after me."

The words hung in the air, his breathing slowed and he turned and walked back to his room.

He sat on the bed, his mind refusing to function and gradually noticed something strange. The backs of his hands and knuckles had bumps on them. He examined them closely, trying to decide if they had been there all his life. He couldn't remember seeing them before. They didn't hurt, they didn't itch, they were just there. Before his eyes, they got bigger, huge, till his hands were double their normal size.

Carefully he got up, walked soundlessly to the door and glided like a shadow with his hands outstretched ahead of him to Mr. Sunder's office.

"Mr. Sunder," he whispered, "look at my hands."

He showed them, his own eyes averted from the grotesque size. Mr. Sunder examined them closely. "Ah yes," he said at last, "quite exciting. I am also having. See," he showed his own hands.

Chris turned his head and looked down at both pairs of hands. Both were completely normal.

"Wonderful," complimented Mr. Sunder. "I am also often feeling bored at night."

Chris returned to his room. As he sat shivering, clutching his head, he felt a peculiar sensation between his thumb and first finger. A pimple had appeared. As he watched, it grew, hesitated, then subsided. As Chris tried to make sense of this, he felt a tingle between his first and middle finger. The same thing happened.

Then one after the other, each subsiding before the next erupted, it happened between all his fingers. He just watched helplessly, till his fingers, as though alien life forms, rose and fell and were still. Then he hit the pillow and didn't wake till noon.

10

When he woke, his head felt clear. Outside he could hear the birds singing. 'I wonder,' he grinned, 'if Delhi birds sing in Punjabi?.

He chortled at the thought. He could almost sense Delhi's winter sun, like a mother's hand on her child, warm and comforting. Then the previous night overcame his mind like a shroud and the sun was darkened and the birds silenced.

He went to the bathroom and examined the mirror. The offending label still clung there, innocuous but threatening. He shaved, had a shower and got ready. 'Wanting to help the Kapoors doesn't seem to be as easy as I thought,' he reflected. 'Maybe I should just get the hell back home.'

There was a knock on his door and Ram Avtar entered. With him was Kalpana.

"Did I wake you?" he asked apologetically.

"Hey, no, sit. Make yourself at home," he urged, not daring to look at Kalpana in case his eyes gave him away. He was breathless.

"I need a real favour from you Chris," said Ram Avtar.

"Hey, sure Mr. K, anything."

"Well, the bank has called again demanding that we pay our dues instantly. They have threatened to seize all our properties. We could get a stay order from the courts preventing them from acting, but it would make all the newspapers and if it became known that we were defaulting, our bargaining position against the union would weaken. So," he asked, "I'm wondering if you could go to Bombay where the bank has its head office. Kalpana's uncle works there and I've spoken to him. He's quite senior there, but he says his position will be greatly strengthened if we could prove that KapCo has a promising future."

"That's where you come in Chris," said Kalpana, not looking at him either.

"Yes," agreed Ram Avtar. "If we can present our foreign collaborator, Kalpana's uncle feels that the bank's board would be persuaded that our future is sound and we are a good bet and deserving of their consideration. I think there should be no problem in re-scheduling our loan after that."

Chris blushed scarlet. "Jeez Mr. K," he pleaded, "I'd be glad to go, but truth is I don't know nothin' about making plastic buckets. Never got around to learning," he explained apologetically.

"No, no", reassured Ram Avtar, " you won't have to say much. Kalpana's uncle just wants to show that you're there. Besides," he added with a genial laugh, "Kalpana will be there to help you along." His laugh boomed.

Chris joined in, not believing his luck. "Gee Mr. K. I really wasn't going to, but gosh, you're a hard man to say no to. Okay," he agreed with utmost reluctance, "you've talked me into it."

"Fine," approved Ram Avtar, "I'll have you booked into the Taj."

"Just one thing, Mr. K," Chris remembered, "I figured may be if we're having so many problems with the factory, have you thought of going into any other kind of business? I mean you could say, 'the hell with this shit' and go into something else."

Ram Avtar shook his head sadly. "Not right now. I've spent my whole life building this. If I am distracted by other

120

work, it will collapse. Besides, what's to stop Prabal Kumar from coming after the workers in the new factory if I do go into something else? If I have been targetted," he reasoned, "I may as well fight it out here."

" Right, right," reassured Chris, "Just thought I'd ask."

They left for Bombay that evening. On the way to the airport, at the departure lounge, on the flight, he and Kalpana didn't exchange a word. He struggled to speak to her, but didn't know what to say. At every opportunity, he gruffly muscled her out of the way and carried her bags for her. In the aircraft for once he was truly grateful for the seats constructed apparently for midgets, because he got to squeeze right alongside her, looking apologetic all the time. The feel of her intoxicated him.

Crowded, boisterous, writhing Bombay left him speechless. As the taxi raced through frenetic streets, he looked at the jampacked shops, the surging masses of people and whistled. "Its party time," he told Kalpana.

She laughed. "In Bombay, always."

That broke the ice and she let him hold her hand. They drove past the sea and Chris grinned happily at it, thinking of some brilliant conversational gambit.

"Nice sea," he ventured.

"Its filthy," she returned, removing her hand.

"Oh no," he cursed.

They checked in and Chris carried his suitcase, hers, his hand bag and hers, ignoring the bell boys. He hoped she'd notice. They went up, she opened a room and Chris eagerly followed. He dumped all the bags on the floor and smiled charmingly. She pushed his bag at him till he picked it up, put a small but firm hand on his back and marched him out. The door shut behind him.

He wandered disconsolately a few doors down till he found one with his number on it. He opened it, picked up his bags and deposited them inside, shut the door and walked further in. Mian Shankar Aiyar sat behind a table in the corner, tinted glasses flashing.

"You're late," he accused.

"Oh, well, you know," faltered Chris, startled, "traffic."

"Did you ask Kapoor?" demanded Aiyar.

"What? Oh yeah. He said 'no'. Wants to fight it out."

Aiyar's lips grew thin. "He must be made to change his mind. When are you meeting Mr. Singh?"

"Who?"

Aiyar sighed audibly. "Kalpana Singh's uncle."

Again Chris was stunned. "Oh, at ten tomorrow morning."

"Refuse to go."

"What? You must be kidding? No way." Chris was outraged.

Without a word Aiyar got up and walked out of the room.

'Whew,' thought Chris, 'thank God that's over. That guy was beginning to spook me.'

Relieved, he decided to go down and explore a little. He hesitated outside Kalpana's door but decided not to push his luck. He went down to the lobby and saw it swirling with people. 'Now they look like they're having a good time,' he thought with approval.

He stepped outside the glass doors and a uniformed chauffeur came upto him with a sign saying "Car for Mr. Shanker."

"Do I look like a Mr. Shanker to you?" laughed Chris

He trotted down the steps and a beggar being wheeled in a cart approached, holding out a can beseechingly, "Shanker, Shanker," he pleaded, "Jai Bhole Shanker".

Chris grimaced and dropped a note into the can. He strode

across the road, looking at a huge gateway and found himself among strollers and families.

A child dashed in front of him, with his mother in hot pursuit. "Shanker," she screamed, "come back here. Shanker!"

Chris began to wonder. 'What the shit is going on?' he mused. 'What's this 'Shanker' stuff?'

He turned towards the sea, worried now, went up to the low wall. A boat beached itself below him just then, drawing his attention. Alongside the bow was written, 'Shanker's Harbour Tours.'

Panic began to mount in Chris again. 'Mian Shanker Aiyar,' he suddenly remembered, starting to sweat. 'My mind's playing tricks' he thought. A few feet away from him, a beggar with a beard beseeched a couple holding hands, "Allah Mian, for the sake of Allah Mian," he intoned.

Chris bolted rapidly for the hotel. In the lobby he paused, wiping the sweat from his face. He saw his hands shaking. He walked to the elevator and got in. It stopped at the next floor and a short and fat man walked in. Chris smelt liquor. Even in his shaken state, Chris thought, 'I've seen him somewhere.'

The door opened at his floor and Chris stepped out. Before the door shut something made him turn. The small man was looking at him intently, his face sweaty. "Courage, Christopher," he said. The door shut.

Numb, Chris walked to his room. Opening the refrigerator, he found an array of beers and began drinking those. He called up room service, ordered a bottle of whisky and some food. He sounded so strange that the operator asked if he was ill.

"Just send it," snapped Chris.

He ate whatever was brought, drank till he fell asleep

and only woke when he felt himself trembling violently as though an unseen hand was shaking him. He managed to pick up the phone and dial Kalpana's room. "I'm sick," he whispered.

She arrived a minute later, with the floor manager who let them in with his key. She felt his forehead. "You're burning," she said.

"What time is it?" he asked.

"Nine", she replied. "You'll have to rest. We'll cancel the appointment."

"No," said Chris trying to control the shivering. "I'll come with you. Get me a doc."

The doctor arrived swiftly and nodded at Chris' instructions. An injection worked miraculously and Chris weakly went to the bathroom to shave. Kalpana helped him get dressed and her concern made him feel doubly heroic.

"Nah, nothing," he assured her bravely. "Just a touch of fever." They were five minutes late for the meeting because they had to wait two hours more in any case.

"This never happens in Bombay," said Kalpana. "They're absolutely business-like here. They respect your time."

Her uncle came out to apologise.

"One of our largest depositors arrived five minutes before you and wants to withdraw ten crores right now," he explained. "We're trying to talk sense into him. Sorry. I hope you'll understand."

Chris was worried because the doctor had warned him that the medicine would stop being effective after two hours. Chris cursed the delay, fearing that the shivering and the fever would return. "Jeez, I walk into that room shaking like a leaf and sweating like a pig and you can say good-bye to any ideas about that loan. Who'd have confidence in a collaborator who looks like he needs all the help he can get himself?" He cursed his luck. But amazingly, the fever didn't return. Nor did the trembling. He began to relax.

"Just leave it to me," he reassured Kalpana.

She looked at him from the corner of her eye. "Leave it to my uncle," she whispered.

Chris was deflated. But when they were invited into the conference room he said a few friendly 'howdys' and nodded pleasantly to anyone around the long table who caught his eye.

Chris and Kalpana were seated at one end while the uncle made a short speech. At one point Kalpana whispered to Chris " Smile" and he beamed enormously, gathering from the glances that the whiz-kid foreign collaborator was being introduced. There were sympathetic nods all around the table, a few questions asked of the uncle and apparently satisfactorily answered and they were ushered out. Neither he nor Kalpana were asked to speak at all.

"Jeez," admired Chris in the taxi, "that was quick. I just wish," he ruminated, "they'd spoken in English."

To his surprise and pleasure, Kalpana leaned her dark head against his shoulder. "Oh Chris," she gasped weakly, "they did."

"Shit," recovered Chris, "you know bankers. Speak their own damn language all of them."

They reached the hotel which had apparently been nearby, though Chris hadn't noticed in his worried state.

"What now?" he asked Kalpana hopefully at her door. "Our flight's in the evening."

"Now" she said, and he felt the familiar hand on his back, "we're going to a poolside party for lunch. Our

125

luggage will get picked up and brought there and then we'll go directly to the airport."

'Such a little thing,' Chris brooded bitterly as he headed once again for his room 'and she has the push of a pile driver.'

They checked out of the hotel and set off once again.

"Bombay people have poolside parties on weekdays at lunch time?" Chris asked.

"The lucky ones," she returned. "Mostly wives."

And so it was. The drive was a long one and they seemed to have left the city when they turned into a side road, went a short distance, behind a screen of trees and parked in front of a rambling old house that had obviously been expensively restored. The sea was visible behind.

"Come on lazy bones," urged, Kalpana, laughing. "We've done our job, now we can party."

She tripped up the stairs and Chris followed behind, watching her longingly. 'Jeez,' he thought, 'if only I hadn't messed up that time.'

They went through the open glass doors into a large airy room scattered with sofas, then onto a patio. Beyond it was a kidney shaped pool and around it a number of women, a few older men and a handful of collegiate looking young men. There were children splashing about at one end.

Kalpana was immediately recognised by what were apparently old friends, with screeches of delight .

'All women screech the same way when they meet after a long time everywhere in the world', thought Chris, 'wonder why?'

He was brooding on this, one of life's eternal verities, as he was introduced to everyone as "Our foreign collaborator." A few women said polite hellos, some shook hands and a few did the *namaste*. 'Always thought it looked like they were praying to me,' Chris pondered. 'Never had women in swimsuits praying to me before, that's for sure.' He thought a bit more. 'Or while wearing anything else for that matter,' he had to confess.

"I'm going for a swim," yelled Kalpana to her friends as she left. "Entertain Chris, okay?" She stopped for a moment . "Not too much entertainment though," she warned.

The women all giggled. "Looks like he could keep us entertained too," one yelled back at Kalpana. They giggled again.

"So," asked another, "how often do you collaborate with the Kapoors?" The women were convulsed.

"I hope," added a third, "you personally help the collaboration get off the ground." They fell about in hysterics.

Chris walked past them with his head held high, but he couldn't resist grinning. 'Women', he thought, 'get them away from men, give them a drink and they're like eagles unchained. They'll rip at anything within reach, but they also soar high,' he had to admit.

He stopped a passing waiter and got a beer. He approached the tables heaped with cuisines of at least five different sorts, including salads, four kinds of meats, a range of vegetarian dishes and naturally about a dozen desserts. He wondered where people had got the notion that Indians barely ate. He'd never seen a country that stuffed itself as much as Indians did. And if they weren't eating meals, they were having what they called 'snacks,' which anywhere else would have qualified as meals, in themselves. Accompanying the snacks was tea. Following tea were drinks. These were invariably followed by more and yet more drinks. All fiercely enjoyed.

As he watched the tables stretching along two sides of the pool, his size attracted some children loitering about.

"Uncle, uncle," they screamed, clustering around him, "how did you get so fat?"

Chris had got used to Indian children announcing instant and intimate relationships with him at first meeting. "Good food," he answered "and weight training."

He picked up one little boy with one hand and lifted him in the air up and down over his head.

With gleeful shrieks the children hurled themselves at him, clambering all over as he lifted and lowered various small bodies on and off the ground, till he looked like a giant tree swaying in the wind with odd shaped objects dangling from every branch.

Eventually he tired and dumped the kids back on the ground to their loud protests.

"Hop it now", he swatted a little boy on his behind.

"Uncle, what else do you do" asked one loiterer as the others reluctantly streamed away voicing their protests.

"I'm a football player," he replied.

"Are you the goal keeper?"

"No, not that kind of football. That's soccer. I play American football."

"What's that?" asked the curious young man.

"That, my dear," drawled a well-bred, haughty, female voice, "is rugby for sissies."

Chris turned and found a lady in her late forties with an Indira Gandhi streak of grey in her hair. She had a long, horsy face, was wearing a black one-piece dress and a cigarette dangled from the finger of one hand and a wine glass was held in the other.

"It has all the illusion of danger," she drawled, "without actually posing any. The current masters of the world are quite adept at such pretence."

The little boy decided that this was all too much for him and left.

Chris wondered whether he should demonstrate a tackle on the lady and then let her decide if there were any dangers in it or not.

She sat down on a chair and crossed her legs. "Tell me, my dear," she purred in a voice so cultured that no human being could have possessed it naturally, "what brings such a distinguished intellectual," she smirked, "to these Third World parts?"

"Work," answered Chris politely, wondering if he could leap fully clothed into the pool and swim a length to get away from her.

"Work, work," she chanted tauntingly, "that's for us of the working class in the Third World, not for our superiors in America."

"And what do you do?" asked Chris aggressively.

"I am part of the Underprivileged Action Collective. We take up the cause of exploited people all over the world."

"Right, what's your husband do?"

She glared suddenly. "He's into manpower exports," she said shortly. Her voice softened. "Be a sweety and get me another drink, will you?"

Chris became a sweety and got her another drink. For a moment he debated whether to open her mouth and stuff the whole thing, alongwith the glass, down her throat, or whether to merely pour it over her head. In the event, he finally just handed it to her.

"How darling of you," she thanked him, "I've always wanted to meet a football player, you know. I think it's really the most typically American of pastimes."

"Yup," agreed Chris, "Sure is."

"So droll," she continued. "With its mix of blood and pageantry and egotism and chivalry, really my dear, its actually Arthurian England masquerading as Hollywood America."

"Right," said Chris, looking ostentatiously at his watch.

"Not that one approves, of course," she hastened to add, "poor dears. You get exploited by the establishment to provide them thrills and spectacles for their edification at the cost of your own blood."

"Without danger of course," reminded Chris.

"Yes," she agreed, heedless. "Its really a nation in a time warp. If only you poor things knew it. One always feels for you people of course and one's heart does so go out to you all."

Chris waved with surprised pleasure to someone behind her and prepared to leave.

"Really, its just a question of raising your self-awareness, you know," she drawled on. "Americans do have such a capacity for self-hypnosis, I'm afraid, but all it needs is the right person and the right vehicle. Now I'm not promising anything, mind you," she cautioned, blowing smoke towards Chris with a patronising smile, "but if the New York Times was to write to me requesting an article on the exploitation of Americans by the establishment, I might, I just might agree, just this once, though no promises, mind you. One stays so busy," she sighed, "but one has to fulfill one's obligations."

"Their letter must be in the mail," assured Chris, waving once again, this time actually at Kalpana emerging from the pool at the other end. "Excuse me, there's my hostess," he fled.

130

Kalpana was drying herself with a towel. Her hair was free of her cap and her body glistened with droplets.

Chris looked at her in her red bikini, her flawless golden brown skin, her perfect figure. He thought frantically of some compliment he could pay her. Something poetic and romantic to reflect his seething emotions. And something that most of all would certainly not offend her.

"Nice ass," he finally blurted.

She buried her face in the towel, then swiftly headed for the house with long strides.

Chris slumped to the ground with a thud. "Shit," he groaned audibly, "I've done it again."

He remained crouched miserably till a servant arrived to inform him that memsahib had already left for the airport and the car was waiting for him.

On the flight back to Delhi she remained with her nose buried in a book. This time Chris cursed the seats. One of his legs remained bent almost permanently, twisted away from all contact with her, the other stuck into the aisle where everybody walking down tripped over it. They glared at him. He glared back, his leg remaining defiantly outflung even after the drinks trolley passed over it.

"You know," he mumbled apologetically, trying to explain to her, "I'm used to cheerleaders."

She remained even more engrossed in her book.

That night he had a severe stomach cramp that wracked him for a minute. As he tried to call on the intercom, it subsided. Two hours later it erupted again for thirty seconds. After that he slept.

11

The next day Ram Avtar was pleased. He kept thanking Chris. "We have bought ourselves time," he said gratefully. "And you were ill too. You are a real friend Chris. You are an Indian at heart."

Chris accepted it for the heartfelt compliment it was meant to be. Besides, Kalpana was sitting there.

"Ajai Vir," Ram Avtar scolded his son, "we have been so busy with our troubles that we have completely neglected Chris. Go have a party this weekend. Have a nice time."

"Well we've been invited to the Gupta's farm tomorrow night," remembered Ajai Vir, "I had declined because I thought you might need me, but I can always call and say I've changed my mind."

"Go, go," urged Ram Avtar, "take a break from all this."

That night Chris was suddenly gripped by anxiety. There was no reason for it, but he was overcome with fear. He woke bathed in sweat, his night clothes so wet that they squelched. He couldn't understand it. He had been to the loctor that day who had pronounced him entirely fit.

"I'm glad all my patients aren't as healthy as you," he had jollied Chris, "I would go broke."

And now here he was, in a cold sweat, worrying, fearing. He reached for the phone. 'But what would I say and to whom? That I'm stricken with anxiety?' He replaced the wet receiver. Sleep came with difficulty.

The next evening they went out of the city. Ajai Vir drove

132

and Kalpana sat beside him. Chris sat in the rear seat, long-
ing for spacious American sedans.

"So what do they grow on this farm?" he asked.

"Nothing, its just a weekend place that its fashionable
to have these days."

Chris nodded. He'd seen some of Delhi's fashions.
'Funny,' he thought, 'back home, I believed being rich in
India meant someone with a bigger hut than his neighbour.
But now, look at the way they live. Servants, chauffeurs,
houses, weekend homes. Jeez, with a bit of money, there is
no life as good as in India. Of course,' he acknowledged,
'without money there is no life as bad as in India too. But
there seem enough people with money.'

They began to bump along a rough track, but Chris
had learned not to pre-judge. Indians built the nicest places,
but it never seemed to occur to them to build equally nice
roads leading to them. And the same people who expected
to invite armies of guests never left space for a single guest's
car to park in their premises. And no one ever seemed
to complain . 'Weird lot,' he thought. 'Nice, but definitely
weird.'

Sure enough, they found cars strewn haphazardly beside the road well before the Gupta's farm. They stuck their
car in an available spot and walked towards the music.

The farm had a wall around it, but through the open gate
Chris could see lights softly shining inside bushes scattered
across the lawn. A bonfire blazed in the middle and huge
speakers blasted the sounds of Indian rap. Figures danced
around the fire.

"Hi Ajai Vir, hello Kalpana," greeted a young man.

"Our host," introduced Ajai Vir, "our friend, Chris."

"Welcome Chris," the host shook his hand, "glad to have

you over. Have a drink," he gestured to the table serving as a bar.

'That should be the motto of the Indian rich,' thought Chris, 'have a drink. I've never met an Indian in his house who hasn't asked me to 'have a drink.' Not,' he conceded, truthful as always, 'that I've ever refused. But I don't even know this guy's name.'

He had got separated from Ajai Vir and Kalpana who were circulating among the guests and exchanging what Chris had learned Indians called 'P.C.'

"Polite conversation," he was told.

He ambled about happily, admiring the house, the tended flower beds, the discreet lighting of table with glows everywhere. There was a long length of table with white table cloth, waiting for the inevitable and huge amounts of food that would weigh it down. He went to the side of the house and found the area behind was wooded with trees.

He returned to the front lawn for another drink and bumped into a girl causing her glass to spill all over the front of her dress.

" Whoops," he apologised, "sorry about that. Can I help clean it up?"

She laughed. "I bet you'd like that. Its okay. It'll dry."

"Fine," said Chris thinking another Indian beauty, "Can we have a P.C.?"

"A what? Oh right," she laughed again, "an Indian P.C." She gave him a speculative look.

"I'm Chris," he introduced himself. "I'm a friend of Ajai Vir Kapoor's. You know him?"

"On sure," said the girl, "vaguely. I'm Amita. What're you doing in India?"

"Oh just some stuff with Ajai Vir's company. I mean

134

their's is just a small company compared to ours," he added casually, "but we like to expand. Its fun."

"What does your company do?" she asked.

"We're into thermo plastics," he answered, whatever that might be.

"And what do you do in it?"

"I'm the Director of International Marketing," he answered shamelessly. "Of course," he added with charming candour, "thats no big deal when your family owns the whole damn company." He laughed heartily but modestly. "Seriously though, its like a real responsibility when you have factories in thirty seven countries. Hell, I'm on a plane most of my life." He laughed again, waving the heavy responsibility away.

"And is this your first visit to India?"

"Yup."

"How d'you like it?"

" Great," he enthused.

"Pretty dirty though," she criticised, "and so backward."

Chris had learned not to fall for that one from Indians. He'd never met people who criticised their country so severely and yet had such a fierce pride in it. "Nah," he contradicted her, "its getting there."

"Yeah? What d'you like about it?"

"Well, the women for one thing. Real special. In fact," he slipped in cunningly, having heard that Indian women had only one thing on their minds — marriage. "I've told my folks, "if I'm going to marry, its going to be an Indian girl, or no one else." He paused expectantly.

"Good for you." she said. "She'll make your life as miserable as a girl from any other country."

'Well, cross that one off my marriage list,' thought Chris.

"And what do you do?" he asked her.

"I'm a fashion designer."

"Really? Who do you work for?"

"Nobody in particular . I free lance."

"Yeah? Does your work take you to the US of A?"

"Just New York sometimes. I go to check out the fashion scene for some of my clients."

"Sounds great. Where do you stay in N.Y?"

"Oh, anywhere near the garment district."

"Gee. We have a company apartment right over there for our visiting executives. Let me know if you need a place to stay any time," he offered generously, "its right on Park Avenue."

"Thats nowhere near the garment district."

Chris cursed a world where you kept meeting people in remote regions who knew more about your own country than you did. "I know that," he fumbled with damage control, "but it isn't that far."

"Yeah," she said shortly. "Oh look, I see someone I know. Nice meeting you. See you later."

'Blew it again,' grimaced Chris, 'Boom'.

She hesitated and came back. She looked closely at his face. "Know what, you look awfully familiar," she said. "What else do you do aside from thermo plastics?"

Chris shrugged. "Played football for the college. You know. American football?"

She said, "Are you Chris Stark?"

"What?" Chris was startled. "Right. Sure. How do you know?"

"Saw your picture in a magazine. You're the linebacker?"

"Jeez," Chris was astounded. "Right."

"Shake," she put out a hand. "I'm nearly a fan."

An astonished Chris shook.

"I'm a real maniac about football," she revealed. "Got addicted during my visits to the U.S." She hooked her arm through his. "So, a real All American." Her breast pressed against his side.

Chris blessed our shrinking world that let strangers become friends so quickly. They began to stroll about, Chris discussing his football triumphs with careful truthfulness, not sure what she might remember. She proved genuinely knowledgeable about the game and its leading personalities.

"The only football player with any brains," she reminded him.

He laughed, embarrassed yet thrilled. 'Jeez,' he marvelled, 'twelve thousand miles from home and you meet someone who knows about you.'

"I may have some brains by football standards," he told her, "but I ain't that great at saying things." It was a fair warning, given his disastrous experiences with Kalpana. "Know what I mean?"

"Right, who is?"

Chris had carefully managed to stroll to the wooded area behind the house and found a bench to sit on. It was dark, with just the moonlight painting the ground silver.

"So," she said, "tell me what it feels like to hit someone. I've never actually met a football player."

"Doesn't feel too bad. Just feels a lot worse when you get hit. How come you got interested in football?"

She shrugged. "I'd never seen anything like it. I grew up watching my brother play cricket and this was as far from that as anything could be."

"That's for sure," grinned Chris. He remembered watching a cricket match on TV and wondering if everybody on the

137

field had died and been buried upright. His arm casually crept along the back of the bench and experimentally touched her shoulder. To his delight she leaned back, her shoulder soft against his arm.

'Touch down,' he exulted to himself.

Then she stood up. "I'll get us both a drink. Be right back." She strode off.

'Now what?' wondered Chris. 'Did I do it again?' He thought some more. 'Nah,' he concluded hopefully. 'She's been to New York. She knows what the score is. She'll be back.'

Suddenly his stomach was seized by a violent cramp and he doubled over in agony. He gasped, squeezing his stomach. The pain subsided. Breathing heavily, he looked up. A man stood in front of him, wearing tinted glasses even at that time of the night. It was Aiyar.

"Ram Avtar," Aiyar spoke quietly but with menace and total command. "He must be made to agree to change his line of business — understand?"

"Do you understand?"

Once again Chris collapsed with a sudden cramp. He felt his body shivering. A fever seemed to singe his brain.

"All right," he pleaded, capitulating completely. "What's happening to me? What do you want him to do? Tell me. Then just leave me to do it alone."

"Make him agree," said Aiyar implacably. "You have millions to gain."

Miraculously all of Chris's ailments disappeared. His breathing returned to normal. "All right," he agreed again. "But how do I get him to agree?"

"Tell him that Stark Industries will give him the money for the new company. We'll make sure you get it. Tell him

138

that you'll set up a chain of shops in the US to which he'll be the sole supplier. He'll have no risk. And you'll both make a lot of money.?"

"What about KapCo?"

Aiyar shook his head. "No compromises with Prabal Kumar. It must stay closed."

"He won't agree."

"Make sure he does. Say Stark Industry's resources will back him fully. He must see that this is his one chance. Tell him not to be sentimental about KapCo. Its dead. But with the new project, he can go international."

"Whats the project?" requested Chris .

"You'll be told." Aiyar's voice hardened. "Make sure he agrees to the new proposal. Don't fail me," he said viciously.

"Okay," hastily agreed Chris, frightened, remembering the pain, the tremblings, the fevers. "Who the hell are you?" he asked in bewilderment.

"I give you two weeks," Aiyar ordered and walked into the woods and was lost from sight.

'Jesus,' thought Chris in complete bafflement, 'the things I get into. What's going on here? Who is this guy? What's happening to me?' He stood up carefully.

'At least I feel fine now,' he thought with relief. 'No pains and fevers or anything. Is it the water or something? Do I have some weird bug? What the hell is going on?'

He saw Amita returning with a glass in each hand "Why Chris, you're looking weak," she exclaimed. "Here, have this. You'll feel better."

He gulped it down and the alcohol soothed him immediately. They both sat down again.

"So" said Amita, nestling against him. "Where were we?" Her hand rested casually on his knee.

Chris took a deep breath, forgot about the recent bewildering minutes and concentrated on the present. He was a strong young man.

"Well," he resumed, "I was going to tell you about the time I made that interception against Notre Dame and ran all the way till their 25 yard line."

"Tell me more," she murmured.

His arm draped itself around her shoulder now quite confidently.

"Well...," he began.

"Chris," he suddenly heard a female voice calling in the distance. "Where are you Chris?"

"Shit," he cursed. It was Kalpana. Hastily Chris and Amita disentangled themselves. Kalpana got nearer and spotted them.

"Here you are," she said. "My, what a cosy gruesome twosome. Who's your new friend Chris?"

"This is Amita," awkwardly introduced Chris. "Kalpana, Ajai Vir's girl friend," he informed Amita. "Amita's like, real interested in football," he earnestly explained to Kalpana.

"Particularly in the dark, I see," sweetly noticed Kalpana.

"Actually," defended Chris, protesting at this calumny, "she's a designer."

"I'm sure she has fabulous designs," said Kalpana with an icy look at Amita, "for everything in pants." She took Chris by the arm. "Come along now," she coaxed him firmly, "we're all having our fortunes told."

He got up reluctantly and Kalpana put her arm around his back to steer him along. "And I'm sure," she cast backwards solicitously to Amita, "that our sporting lady friend will soon find some new footballs to play with in the dark."

She hustled Chris away.

They went into the house and found the living room full of people . In the middle, on the floor sat an oriental looking man with a sheaf of paper slips in front of him. He was dressed in an orange robe of coarse cloth and had a smiling look of great calm on his face.

"He's a Tibetan fortune teller," explained Kalpana. "The Guptas have tried him out earlier and they swear by him. He just turned up out of the blue and we're lucky to be around. He uses some ancient Tibetan method with those bits of paper."

"How does it work?" asked Chris curiously.

"Well I'm told he senses the vibrations in each person and then pulls out one of those pieces of paper. It has a message that only the person concerned can understand."

"In Tibetan?"

"Yeah, but he reads it in English."

Chris looked sceptical, "I don't believe this astrology shit, you know. Its just a pile of junk."

"Maybe," laughed Kalpana in agreement, "but its great fun. Do you want to try it? Its free."

"Why the hell not?" shrugged Chris. He waited till the next person was through, then sat on his haunches in front of the cross-legged Tibetan. 'How do all these guys sit for so long like that?' he wondered. 'My legs would never straighten again.'

The Tibetan silently held out his hand and Chris placed his own on it. The monk shook his head. "Right hand," he instructed.

Chris did as told and the Tibetan shut his eyes, concentrating on the sensation of Chris' palm on his own. With his left hand he riffled through the slips of paper repeatedly. Suddenly he stopped and pulled out a slip. His eyes opened as he read it

"Faustus," he read, "Remember Dr. Faustus."

He removed his hand and motioned for the next person to replace Chris.

Chris was thunderstruck. "Wow," he said in astonishment to Kalpana. "This shit works."

"I told you," she said. "It only has meaning for that person. Who was Faustus?"

"My old buddy," exclaimed Chris. "LeRoy Faustus Jones, greatest running back in our team's history. 'Fast Faustus' the papers called him." He gave a clenched fist black power salute to the monk. "All right" he exclaimed. "Thats some great shit you got going," he complimented. "Wasn't no doctor though, thats for sure. Could just about sign his name, old Faustus."

"Maybe," said a voice quietly behind him, "it was some other Faustus."

He turned and it was Amita waiting for her turn with the monk.

"Oh hi," said Chris. "Which other?"

"I think," butted in Kalpana, "our lady friend with the footballs is referring to the legend of Dr. Faustus."

"Who's he?" asked Chris. "What'd he do?"

Kalpana explained. "He sold his soul to the devil in return for everything he ever wanted in life. Then the devil came back and claimed his forevermore. Its an old play by Christopher Marlowe. I don't think," she added scathingly, looking everywhere except at Amita, "that Mr. Marlowe had hopeful she-devils in mind though, trying to claim souls or whatever, for one night stands."

Once again she swept Chris off.

"Aren't you getting your fortune told?" protested Chris.

"Later," she said, steering him out to the front lawn, "later."

The bonfire had burned low and now emitted a fitful radiance. A slow number was playing. She came into his arms. "Let's dance," she murmured.

Chris felt a leap of warmth and held her tight. "Where's Ajai Vir?"

"Gone home. He got tired. The Guptas will get us dropped back."

Chris put his face in her hair and breathed in woman smells. As often happens in such cases and at such times, he felt weak kneed .He felt her softness all along his body and held her closer. The darkness around embraced them comfortingly and he crushed her hard to himself, barely moving.

The number ended and a loud Baba Sehgal rap song that Chris recognised came on. Reluctantly he separated from Kalpana, glaring at the giant speaker. 'If I ever meet that Baba guy,' he promised in unspoken fury to the speaker, 'I'll break him in two.'

Kalpana began moving away. "Ladies room," she told him. "Just be back."

Chris went to the bar, got a drink and moodily surveyed the dancers who were now enthusiastically howling along with the song. 'No luck,' he muttered bitterly to himself. 'No damn luck in this country at all. Damn Indian singers. Why couldn't they stick to yodelling or whatever the hell it is they do. Who told them to sing rap? Break his face,' he swore silently.

The next song was another slow one and Chris perked up instantly. He set off in search of Kalpana. He went to every room in the house, knocking at all the bathroom doors but there was no sign of her. He finally seized a passer-by by arm.

"Hey buddy," he asked, "any other rooms in this place?"

"Upstairs," pointed the man, "the *barsati*."

Chris found a staircase going up and climbed. He opened a door and stopped in shock at the sight. A tall but skinny man was cringing in the corner, his hands trying to shield his face, while Kalpana attacked him with a pillow.

"Hey!" exclaimed Chris striding forward. "Cut that out now. What's got into you? Who's this guy?" He used one massive arm to gently pull Kalpana back.

"Tried to get fresh with me," panted Kalpana, giving the man a kick. "Creep."

"Hush now," Chris pulled her out of striking distance. "He what?"

"Tried to kiss me." She flung the pillow at him. "Stupid drunk. Lech," she abused.

Chris let go of her and headed for the man lolling drunkenly in the corner. He grabbed him by the shirt front and effortlessly raised him till his feet were six inches off the floor.

"Yo," said Chris, "you acting funny with my girl?"

"Its not my fault," mumbled the man, "I'm from Patna *yaar*." Chris shook him roughly.

"But," protested the man again, "I'm from Patna *yaar*." Chris gave him a slap.

"Come on, *yaar*," beseeched the man, "you live in Delhi. You can get all the girls you want. But I'm from Patna *yaar*."

Chris gave him another slap.

144

"Oh let him be Chris," Kalpana tried to pull him away. "He's just drunk."

Chris gave him a last slap and let him go. The man collapsed into a corner and lay slumped.

They walked out. "I wasn't too hard on him, was I?" worried Chris suddenly "Weedy little fucker. Do you think I've killed him?"

"No," reassured Kalpana, good humour restored, clutching his arm, giggling and batting her eyes at him. "Saved me from a fate worse than death. My hero."

Chris grinned too. "Damn right." He thumped his chest.

They went back to the living room where the Tibetan was still holding court. 'Dr. Faustus?' wondered Chris, 'what in hell did he mean?'

They watched the monk for a while and Chris wondered whether to ask him to elaborate.

"I need a drink after that," Kalpana slipped away. "I'll get it from the kitchen."

After a minute Chris decided to get a drink too and also headed towards the kitchen. When nearly there he heard a shriek and quickly pushed open the swinging door.

Kalpana stood alone near the counter, one hand on her rear.

"What happened?" asked Chris.

"It was the guy from Patna," she complained. "I was getting my drink and he pinched my bottom."

"Jeez, what a fanatic. Which way did he go?" demanded Chris.

She pointed towards the back door leading to the trees. "That way."

Chris strode out. "This time he's had it," he promised. "Patna or no Patna."

He stepped into the cool night and walked to the tree line. He prowled along the trees, peering intently to see if he could spot the guy hiding anywhere. He walked up and down several times, but it was too dark and there was no sign of him. 'Gone into hiding,' he thought in disgust, giving up. He turned to return to the house and went a few steps when something made him look back.

A figure stood there just in front of a tree.

It was the Latin American he had seen in the Oberoi and Taj elevators. His face was absolutely white in the moonlight. His eyes showed a man on the verge of total collapse. His mouth opened.

"Faustus, Chris," he whispered, but Chris heard him clearly, 'Remember Dr. Faustus."

"I want to talk to you," said Chris. "What's this Faustus crap?" He started towards the man.

A sudden disturbance a little away made him look. It was the guy from Patna emerging from the trees, the leaves crackling under him.

"Hey you," Chris changed direction and charged for him. "I want you." The man melted back into the woods. "And you wait there," Chris yelled over his shoulder at the Latino, then slowed puzzled. He had disappeared. When he looked in front, the man from Patna was gone too. The woods were absolutely silent. Chris barged into them and thrashed about, but found no one.

He went back shaking his head. 'Jeez. Weird stuff. What's going on?' He found Kalpana in the living room. "Did you catch him?" She asked.

He shook his head. "I want to talk to you," he gestured her over and went to the backyard again.

146

Obediently she followed. They sat on the bench he'd shared with Amita.

"Tell me about this Faustus stuff," he asked. "What's the story on that?"

"Why?"

"Trying to figure out what the monk meant."

She laced her fingers through his and told him whatever she remembered from her college days. "Basically just about what I told you. The devil meets Dr. Faustus and asks him what are the things he most dreams of getting in life. Faustus tells him and the devil says he can have them all for a year, but after that year, he'll come back and possess Dr. Faustus' soul for eternity. Dr. Faustus agrees and for a year he has the greatest time anyone could imagine. Then when the year is nearly over, he changes his mind. But its too late. The devil arrives and carries him away." She looked puzzled. "What could it possibly have to do with you?"

"Beats me," said Chris. "say, do you believe in the devil and stuff like that?"

"Don't be silly Chris," she chided. "We're all adults here."

"Sure, sure," hastened Chris. "But has anything weird ever happened to you? I mean ghosts and stuff like that? This is India you know, its supposed to be full of mysteries and shit."

"Oh come off it Chris," she snapped. "What's got into you? We're a progressive, forward looking, modern country that's launching its own satellites and rockets. We don't have time for ghosts and nonsense. We're going to be the super power of the next century." She pulled her hand away and stood up. "Lets go home."

As the Gupta's car with its sleepy chauffeur turned into the highway, a truck thundered down. They stopped to let it pass. Behind it Chris read. "Forget me not." And under it, "Aiyar Transport Company."

12

The next morning Chris was still asleep when there was a knock on his door. They had returned nearly at dawn and he woke with great difficulty. Finally he roused himself.

"Come in," he growled hoarsely.

The door opened and Ajai Vir stood there fully dressed.

"Hi," croaked Chris. "Come on in. What time is it?"

"Nearly noon. Did you have a nice time?" Ajai Vir sat down on a chair.

"Great," said Chris. "one of the world's best kept secrets is that Indians are the greatest party givers. You have an aspirin? I think I have a hangover."

Ajai Vir picked up the intercom extension and asked for the aspirin.

"Did you eat enough" he asked. "You should line your stomach before drinking."

"Christ, I forgot completely. What's up? How are things going?"

"Terrible. I'm worried about Dad," said Ajay Vir. "I think he's given up."

"Nah, don't worry about him," reassured Chris, "he's a real scrapper."

"Well, all he's doing is praying. Looking for some way to make the minister smile. Praying is not going to get us out of this mess. Look Chris," Ajay Vir pulled his chair forward, "saving this company is upto us now. With all respect, my dad can't handle it anymore. It's beyond him."

Chris again remembered Aiyar. "Why don't you just get out of this business and start another one?" he asked Ajay Vir. "No big deal. People open and close businesses all the time in America. You know that."

Ajay Vir shook his head. "Can't afford to Chris. Everything we have is sunk in KapCo."

"Hell, we'll help you," urged Chris. "Don't forget, I'm officially an Indian at heart now," he reminded. "We'll put up the money, you make the stuff and ship it to us. That's it."

Again Ajay Vir refused. "Dad'll never agree," he said. "Not at least till there's still a chance of rescuing KapCo. It's not just a business for him, you know, Chris. It's his life. I guess it's hard for us to understand. We've never put so much of ourselves into anything. But after Mom died, KapCo became his obsession." Ajay Vir's voice took on a tinge of bitterness. "He once told me that I was his only child, but the business came first."

"Don't feel too bad," sympathised Chris. "My old man made it on his own too. And I think he often forgets he has a kid. Not that I've been of much help to him."

"Well," confessed Ajay Vir, "tell you the truth, neither have I. But this is the time to come good. What do you say? Are you in?"

"Hey pardner", protested Chris, "you couldn't keep me out. Let's go for it."

There was a knock and Tai entered with an aspirin. Chris gulped it down.

"So," he asked, "what do we do?"

"Well, I've been thinking," said Ajay Vir "and I feel that even if the business is closed, there's no reason why the three B's can't be used in this situation. Actually," he admitted, "I can't think of anything else. Business school doesn't exactly prepare you to cope with the Prabal Kumars and Sevak Chands of this world."

"I forget now," tried to recollect Chris. "What were the three B's again?"

"Butter them, Bash them, or Bribe them."

"Right. So what do we start with?"

"Butter them, I guess," suggested Ajay Vir. "May be if we can pretend to be nice to Prabal Kumar, he'll get off our case."

"Shit. I'd rather be nice to an alligator."

"I know. How d'you think I feel?" answered Ajay Vir. "But we've got to play it cool and outsmart the son of a bitch."

"Right," conceded Chris. "Let's try it out. How d'you figure to butter him up?"

"Say good things about him in the press, I guess. He's bound to hear about it."

Chris thought, "Yeah," he agreed. "Let's call your journalist friends and get something printed."

"There's a problem there though," said Ajay Vir, "I got all of them to cover the time we sent in Lal Verma's workers. And they all know what happened. Now if I suddenly call up singing Prabal Kumar's praises, they'll think I've gone nuts or something."

"Yeah," Chris agreed. "How do we do it then?"

They both thought about it.

"Beats me," finally concluded Ajay Vir.

"Well, hold on a minute," said Chris. "I don't know if it'll work here, but I've got me an idea." He paused, gathering his thoughts." You know, back home, whenever we needed publicity, we never called any journalist directly.

Don't think my Dad even knows any. He just hires a PR agency and they bring down a bunch of guys from the papers and take them around the plant and talk to Dad and stuff. I don't know. You have those PR companies here too?" he asked.

Ajay Vir's eyes lit up. "Yes we do. I can find out which is a good one. Chris, my man," he walked over and they slapped hands, "that is a pure gold idea. We're businessmen now buddy, real businessmen."

He left to find out more and Chris dozed till lunch. In the evening they went out to meet the person from the public relations agency Ajay Vir had called after a friend recommended it.

"Why don't you call the guy home?" Chris had enquired.

"Don't want Dad to know. We'll just sort this problem out and hand him the whole thing nicely worked out and neatly tied with a ribbon. And screw the minister and his smile."

"Yeah," sneered Chris. "We'll show them."

They went to the Chinese restaurant at the Taj Hotel. "This is where Delhi's business deals get done," explained Ajay Vir. "It's the right place for a serious discussion."

"Great," agreed Chris, looking around as they waited to be seated. "Nice."

The hostess greeted Ajay Vir and he gave his name.

"We have reservations," he said.

"Yes sir. Your guests are waiting for you," she led the way.

They went to a table for four along the wall and a man and a woman who had been sitting there got up.

The woman was dressed in a sari, was nice looking, with close cropped hair. The man was short with a French beard and a moustache and wore a suit. He looked earnest yet wise.

"Good evening, Mr. Kapoor, evening sir." he greeted Chris. "I'm Satish Shah, my colleague, Ms. Kumari."

They all shook hands and murmured hellos. Drinks were ordered, the menu scanned and decided upon, the drinks seized and started with and then they got down to serious business.

"Do you mind if I smoke sir?" asked Shah proffering a packet.

They declined but Ms. Kumari took one and lit up. So did Shah.

"Tell me sir," he encouraged, "what's the problem here? We've done some brainstorming at the office already." He let this sink in with a brief smile "and I've read the clips we have on KapCo. Oh yes," he assured them waving his cigarette, "we keep files on all the important companies." He let that sink in too. Ms. Kumari nodded. "And we've agreed that what KapCo needs at this point in time is a positive image projection. We need to get the public's mind off the strike and on to the potential earnings extrapolated for the next three years." He looked keenly at them. "Have a whole series of articles on KapCo's market penetration, rural reach and most of all, profit potential. The last of course," he smiled a roguish man to man smile, "will be provided by us. I already have people making the bar charts to supply to the newspapers to accompany the articles. They never do these things on their own. But" he reassured them, "we'll organise a series of interviews with the main publications and I will personally accompany the journalists for the interviews with KapCo's key executives and naturally with your distinguished father. These journalists are of

153

course," he paused significantly and smiled knowingly yet briefly again "oh, good friends of ours. In fact I spoke to some of them just before I came here and requested them to be on stand by."

Ms. Kumari nodded intelligently.

There was a long pause as Ajai Vir digested all this. "Well, actually," he said, hesitating as to how to phrase it, "we just want some articles written saying nice things about Prabal Kumar. Board decision," he added.

"Just what I was thinking," smoothly agreed Mr. Shah, looking significantly at Ms. Kumari. "A whole range of features detailing his background, his rise to power and his significant contribution to peaceful industrial relations. Perfect for KapCo", he applauded.

"Why?" asked Ms. Kumari.

Shah glared at her and she hastily lit another cigarette.

"Well, I'm sure we can leave the details of the articles to you," said Ajai Vir, "just make sure I'm quoted in them. But my father is not to even be told about this project, much less asked for and interviewed."

"Obviously," said Shah, much surprised that Ajay Vir would even need to mention it. "That's just what I said when we were doing a meeting on the KapCo situation at the office. 'It's the younger generation that has to call the shots,' I said. 'The old guard's out. Finito."

"Yeah okay," agreed Ajai Vir.

They began to dig into the food that had been served.

"Great stuff," enthused Chris.

Mr. Shah recommenced a non-stop flow of the utmost inanity about the nation, its problems and the solutions, which apparently lay with public relations.

"The reason India is in such trouble," he explained,

"is because we've forgotten our roots, the independence movement. This was really an organised effort at public relations. That's right," he nodded with significance and sagacity, one more little smile playing about his lips. "Gandhi was a PR man."

Ms. Kumari nodded intelligently again.

Nothing of equal significance occurred during the rest of the dinner and they went home.

Over the next few days Mr. Shah actually performed and a few journalists turned up and with a breathtaking indifference, noted down Ajai Vir's lavish praises of Prabal Kumar. These appeared in decidedly obscure journals, but were noted with astonishment by the union leader. However, he ignored them. Ram Avtar had them pointed out to him, grimaced, but said nothing.

He had aged visibly. That ruddy face had become grey, he had lost weight, the versatile laugh that had so captivated clients and demoralised competitors, didn't boom any more. His energetic walk was still evident, but it was obviously a forced one. He spent more and more time in prayer and one day Ajai Vir opened his father's bedroom door to find him lying full length in front of his temple, his arms stretched in front, clasped together.

Frightened, Ajay Vir feared he might have collapsed, but then saw Ram Avtar's lips moving and realised he was praying, with tears streaming down his face. So engrossed was he that he didn't notice Ajai Vir enter or quietly leave, silently shutting the door behind him.

After seeing this, the young man made a decision.

"Chris," he told his friend, "buttering Prabal Kumar hasn't worked. There's been no response to the articles. It's been a waste of whatever I paid to the PR agency. And I'm telling you Chris, if KapCo goes my Dad'll just die. He wouldn't survive it," Ajay Vir heaved a sigh. "So I've decided to move to the second 'B.' "

"Which one?" asked Chris.

"Bash them," answered Ajay Vir grimly.

"I'll do it," rejoiced Chris right away. "Lemme at him. I can take him."

"No, no," silkily remonstrated Ajay Vir," it's got to be done cunningly. So it can't be traced back to us. I mean let's face it Chris," he objected. "If a 6 ft. 5 inch foreigner knocks the blocks off Prabal Kumar, how long would it take people to figure out who it was?"

"Good point," agreed Chris, "But man, it really burns me up. I could really fry that guy's ass."

"We'll do it too," promised Ajay Vir, "but not with our own hands."

"Who've you got in mind then?"

"A hit man."

"Like, in the Mafia?" Chris was incredulous.

"Yeah. The Indian Mafia."

"Wow," Chris whistled. "I dunno Ajay Vir," he objected dubiously. " I mean some of those guys are really bad news. You know, like really mean mothers."

"No sweat," assured Ajay Vir with complete confidence, "I can handle them."

"You actually know somebody?"

"Sort of. A friend of a friend's told me about this guy. He's the best in the business. I mean when he goes after somebody, that guy's gone. And I do mean gone for good."

"And this guy'll like, take on the job."

"We'll make him an offer," Ajay Vir said with a steely look, "that he can't refuse."

The next night they set off to find the hit man, Ajay Vir having received directions from his friend's friend. These did not prove to be very clear and they spent several hours bumping around in a part of Delhi neither had seen before. They had hired a 'rent your own car' since Ajay Vir had planned the entire operation meticulously.

"The POA," he had explained sinisterly to Chris, "is as follows."

"The what?"

"POA. Plan of Action."

"Right. All right."

"First we hire this taxi so that even if someone takes down the number they can't trace it back to us. Then we meet Bhola."

"Who?"

"The hit man. His name's Bhola Prasad."

"Yeah, okay."

"We give Bhola fake names, so even if he gets caught by the cops, they'll never be able to find out who we are."

"Good plan," acknowledged Chris in admiration. "But what about me? He'll know I'm not an Indian."

But Ajay Vir had not done an MBA for nothing. He had thought of that too. "I'll pass you off as an Armenian."

"A who?"

"An Armenian. They're big and white too. It's in the CIS. And there's so much havoc going on in Armenia right now, that even if the Indian police tries to trace you there through Interpol, or whatever, nobody'll be able to get any information out of that place. I mean it's in shambles. Who'll have time to go around chasing after some guy who doesn't even exist?" he asked logically.

157

"You think Interpol might get into this?" Chris was beginning to have doubts.

"Could well be," Ajay Vir replied with a shrug. "Let's be clear on this Chris. When Prabal Kumar gets blown away, the shit'll really hit the fan. But we can take care of that. We'll just make sure we've covered our tracks."

Chris's sense of uneasiness mounted, but it was too late to back out. "But won't this guy want to know why we want to get Prabal?" he asked.

Ajay Vir tapped the table in triumph. "That's the best part," he said. "We'll say we're drug smugglers. You from Armenia and me from Bangladesh and Prabal has double crossed us on a deal. And," he added as an inspired after thought, "raped our sisters. So even if the cops catch Bhola, and he sings, they'll all be running around looking for the drug angle. We'll be home and free. Hell," he added excitedly as another thought occurred to him, "even if the police don't catch Bhola, we'll make an anonymous phone call and tell them. They'll grab him and make him talk." He thought intently for a bit. "Well, he may not initially talk, Chris —you know, there's a peculiar sense of honour among these criminal types. He'll feel that he's eaten our salt and all that crap, but the cops'll make him speak. Man," he enthused, "those cops are some mean dudes, I can tell you."

They both laughed in pleasure at the prospect of what the cops would do to Bhola. Chris keenly examined the plot from every angle and like Ajay Vir, could find no flaw in it.

"Can't fail," he concluded admiringly.

"Betcha." Ajay Vir and Chris slapped palms and went out and bought dark glasses.

And now they were bumping around some god-forsaken

colony with rutted roads and new buildings that already looked like derelict monuments, blackened by the ages and crumbling. Most seemed empty.

"We've gone past this place twice before." complained Chris. "Can't anyone give us directions?"

They had stopped various people still on the street and asked for the address. The moment they heard the name of the person, their helpfulness vanished and they denied all knowledge of his existence and hurried away.

Just then they spotted a policeman in uniform wobbling along on a bicycle and blew the horn vigorously and waved at him. He swerved and peddled over and stopped beside them.

"Where is the Garib Society office please?" asked Ajay Vir.

The policeman had a kind, weather beaten face and looked tired. He examined them closely for a while and then shrugged. He pointed to a narrow alley going between two buildings just opposite them.

"Inside there," he said briefly, pedalling off. He didn't look back at them again.

"Goddamn," swore Ajay Vir, as they got out of the car and locked it, "We've asked people for directions who were standing right at the alley and they claimed they didn't know."

They entered the alley which was dimly lit and narrow. They stumbled along for a while till they saw a door set in the wall ahead. Above, it said, "Garieb Sossety."

"Look at that spelling," whispered Ajai Vir

They grunted in amusement.

A small window to their right suddenly opened and a man's face was framed there.

"What do you want?" he asked harshly.

"We have come to meet Bholaji," replied Ajay Vir, his heart beating fast.

"There is no one here by the name. Please leave," the face demanded.

Ajay Vir was incensed. "He may not be there," he snapped back, "but he lives here," he pointed to the door in front.

"Who has sent you?" demanded the man again.

"That is only for Bholaji to know," retorted Ajay Vir.

"Who are you?" he asked offensively.

The man stared at them for a while and the window was slammed shut.

They waited uncertainly.

"What does Garib Society mean?" whispered Chris.

"It means Society for the poor."

"Jeez, you sure we're at the right place?"

The door in front opened and a man beckoned them in. They entered a dingy, small, but stark hall and the man pointed to a door on the left. Ajay Vir opened it and they went inside. It was well lit, though windowless. It was completely bare expect for a table, some rickety chairs on one side of the table and a cushioned chair on the other side. They sat down, examined the room, saw nothing to examine, looked at each other and shrugged.

"I really think we've come to the wrong place," whispered Chris again. "This doesn't look like much. I mean no guns or anything. Should be something."

The door behind them opened and shut again and a man brushed past them and went and sat on the cushioned chair. He was tall, Ajay Vir noticed, dressed in the coarse white kurta and trouser pyjamas of the Indian politician. He was extremely well built, with a hard face covered with a closely cropped but rough beard and moustache that joined his side burns. A prominent nose gave him a fierce look along with dark and unfathomable eyes. His hair was cut so close that it just about covered his scalp. He held a packet of State Express cigarettes and a box of matches in one hand which he put on the table.

'He'd be a tough customer in a fight,' thought Chris.

"Yes please?" His voice was guttural but neutral. His eyes were examining them very closely.

Suddenly Ajay Vir felt completely inadequate and foolish. His courage drained out. 'This was not a very good face,' he thought, 'This guy looks dangerous. What the hell was I thinking of?'

He looked down at the table in misery and there was a long silence.

The man had finished examining them and Ajay Vir heard him strike a match. He smelled the aroma of tobacco.

'Shit,' he thought, 'I must have been mad. I've got to get out of here.'

He removed his dark glasses and spoke, "Nothing much," he said lamely, " I just heard that the Garib Society does a lot of good work, so since my friend and I were passing this way, we thought we would just meet you and see how your work was going."

A light gleamed momentarily deep inside Bhola's eyes as the cigarette smoke trickled out of his nostrils. He was completely impassive otherwise.

"Anyway," concluded Ajay Vir miserably, "it was a nice feeling meeting you and we'll meet again."

He stood up, much to the bewilderment of Chris, who hadn't understood a word since the conversation was in Hindi. But he meekly followed Ajai Vir as he headed out.

They went down the corridor and Ajai Vir was fumbling with the front door trying to find a handle or a bolt or something to open it, when he felt a hand on his shoulder.

It was Bhola and he was smiling. His teeth were stained red with betel juice, but it was a genuine smile. His whole face had softened.

"Guests who have come to my humble home," he declared firmly, "cannot leave without a cup of tea."

He put a paternal arm around both of them and guided them back. "Do come in," he urged, "do come in."

Unresisting, they went back and sat again.

"Ramu," yelled Bhola, "get three teas."

He opened his cigarette packet and offered it. "Do take, do take," he requested good naturedly. Intimidated, relieved, Ajay Vir took one. Bhola lit it for him and then lit his own.

"It's a good thing I was able to meet you today. I am out so often that I am rarely here," Bhola chatted. "You know what a politician's life is." He smiled and there was a real amusement in it. "I always say, 'it's no life, it's all politics.' Did you have any difficulty finding this place?"

"Why yes. No one seemed to know where it was," complained Ajay Vir.

Bhola sighed. "I keep putting up signs and the urchins keep stealing them. What do I do?" he asked helplessly.

"You're a politician?" asked Ajay Vir in perplexity.

"Yes. M.L.A. Elected twice from this constituency." He couldn't resist boasting . "People say I'm unbeatable here. But I say 'I'm not the one who is unbeatable, it is my work in my constituency that is unbeatable'."

"What party are you with?" asked Ajay Vir.

"Independent. But I am thinking of joining the Congress.

I am not keen, but they are after me to join. What do you think?" he asked, pouring out the tea into small cups. "Is it better to keep your independence, or to be with a party?"

"Well," said Ajay Vir, thawing at this man about whom he had clearly been misguided. " If you're with a Party, then at least you'll have their backing if you want to do something for your constituency, otherwise you have no clout."

Bhola waved his finger in agreement. "That's what I've found too. If you're not with a party, nobody listens !" he exclaimed. "All my constituency work gets stopped because I have no power. I tell you, it's really the limit," he protested. "All that politicians want is power. Nobody is even thinking about the nation."

Ajai Vir couldn't have agreed more. He held forth with his views on politicians and clearly he and Bhola had hit it off very well. Somewhere along the way he introduced himself and Chris... with their real identities... which didn't seem to surprise his new found friend at all. Ajai Vir poured out his heart about KapCo and Bhola sympathised completely. There was something very reassuring and trustworthy about him, felt Ajai Vir.

"Yes," Bhola commiserated, "I have read about that Prabal Kumar. He is just," he said in disgust, "a power hungry politician."

"Not just that," burst out Ajai Vir, "he's also corrupt. "He wants," he revealed in horror, "money to end the strike."

Bhola looked shocked and amazed. "No, no," he said "that I have never heard of him. Is such a thing possible?"

"Never heard," jeered Ajai Vir, "I'm telling you, it's just a game of money. Do you know how much he wants to end the strike? Think," he urged Bhola, "guess how much he wants?"

Bhola's face was completely non-committal, but his hands made helpless gestures.

"Fifteen crores," swore Ajai Vir. "Can any sane person imagine that? Fifteen crores! Has his family seen that kind of money in fifty generations?"

A strange light of understanding had begun to burn in Bhola's eyes.

"We just don't know what to do," confessed Ajai Vir, pouring his little heart out. "We are about to finish off. I could even say we're already finished."

A succession of lights were now racing in Bhola's eyes, like those of an aircraft taking off in the dark, but abruptly he extinguished them.

"No, no," he reassured Ajai Vir, "Don't be afraid." He pointed upwards. "Have faith in the chap with the blue umbrella."

"Blue umbrella?" Ajai Vir was astonished. "Ah! God!" he exclaimed. "You mean, have faith in God! My father's trying that too," he lamented. "It's not working. The only thing that will work with Prabal Kumar," he swore savagely, "is if we get a gun..."

"No, no," abruptly interrupted Bhola with alarm. "God is there. God is great. He is very kind hearted. Every thing is his. We are just tenants who live in his house and use what he loans us for a while. He looks after us all. Pray to him and have faith in him. My own experience is that he looks after everything and when his hand is on us, all is well. That is how I have done a little bit in life."

Ajai Vir sighed and bent down and soon the conversation petered out.

"Well, we have taken a lot of your time," said Ajai Vir looking at his watch. "We should go now."

164

They stood up and with exquisite courtesy Bhola escorted them to their car and held the door open for Ajai Vir. They all shook hands, promising to meet again and Ajai Vir and Chris drove off.

"So," Chris asked, 'what was that all about? Is he going to do it or what?"

Ajai Vir roared with laughter. "He's no mafia hood," he chortled, "he's a good guy. Christ," he wondered, "the things people make up about politicians. No wonder they go and get a bad reputation. Endless bloody stories."

13

In the following days, Ajai Vir recovered his confidence. After his excellent meeting with Bhola and after seeing his father's continually declining state, he felt renewed in his determination to have Prabal Kumar killed. He felt that politicians in general, except for Sevak Chand, were unnecessarily maligned and many of them were basically sweet chaps. He felt that people like Bhola Prasad who only wanted power to serve their constituencies better, were simply unsuited to the grim and nasty business of eliminating snakes like Prabal Kumar. "What we need," Ajai Vir told Chris, "is not a politician, but a thug."

"Right," agreed Chris, apparently able to see the difference.

Ajai Vir, therefore sent word to his friend's friend, complaining bitterly about having been guided to a nice, religious minded guy who could barely find time to come home after exhausting himself all day in bettering the lives of his constituents. Ajai Vir demanded directions to a better class of assassin.

Having recovered from his shock at hearing Bhola Prasad so described, the friend's friend, since he was basically possessed of a kind heart, wrote down the name and address of a lower class thug and sent it.

Ajai Vir sighed with delight when he read the address.

"I know of this place," he said tapping the paper in satisfaction. "It's where they add lepers' piss to illicit hooch to sell to the poor. Gives an added kick," he explained to Chris.

Confident that the right kind of gentlemen would reside in such a neighbourhood, they set off again.

It was afternoon and they had a long drive half way down New Delhi. They kept on the Ring Road interminably, and somewhere just after the cremation grounds, they turned and bumped down.

"Another Indian speciality," thought Chris in discomfort. "Get off the highway and you bump."

They parked alongside the road and got off.

"It's around here," Ajai Vir told Chris. "We'll have to find it." He had his dark glasses back on.

They walked along the track and came within sight of the Yamuna river. On the right was a clutter of huge pipes and black tarpaulins shaped into tents. Stones anchored the tents to the ground. Smoke rose from a dozen little fires and mingled with the smell of excreta.

"This is it," recognised Ajai Vir, "I've seen pictures."

"What are the pipes?" asked Chris.

"People live in them."

As they picked their way towards the shanties, they found a man sprawled on the ground. "Doped," informed Ajai Vir. "Lots of peddlers here."

The inevitable children appeared and Chris wondered if there was just one group of bedraggled, unhealthy and loud children who followed him about everywhere, springing up in his path whenever he went for a walk, or whether the whole country was actually swimming with them. They formed a tugging, Praetorian guard and accompanied the duo.

Ajai Vir stopped in front of a woman squatting and stirring a cauldron over a fire.

"Where is Mirchi?" he asked.

The woman took the ladle out of the tub, wiped it on the edge and gestured at the largest tent.

They went towards it and a man lying on a cot outside got up immediately. Dressed in a *dhoti* and dirty undershirt, he looked at them with hostile curiosity.

"Call Mirchi" ordered Ajai Vir authoritatively.

The man disappeared inside the tent and came out a moment later. Behind him stood Mirchi. Chris and Ajai Vir exchanged startled glances. Mirchi was a woman.

Short, squat, her arms covered with silver bangles, dressed in a black skirt and blouse inlaid with small mirrors, pock-marked, her dark skin contrasting with her mouth stained red with *paan*, she was aware of their consternation. She spat out a stream of *paan* juice at the ground.

"Yes?" she demanded. It was an uncouth, grating voice.

"We have work with you," stated Ajai Vir. "Where should we sit?"

She gestured to the cot the man had been occupying and they gingerly seated themselves on it.

She sat on a rock near them, her legs sprawled. She looked at them directly for the first time and her eyes were narrow, cunning and completely black.

"If you want a woman," she spat again , the red squirt exploding off the ground, "go to that tent." She nodded at one. "We can bring boys also, but that costs more. Sometimes the rich people like hermaphrodites, but for that you will have to come back in the evening." She picked a piece of something between her teeth and wiped it on the rock.

"It is other work," said Ajai Vir irritatedly.

"For *charas* you will have to come with a recommendation. The CID people are always troubling us."

"This is important work," said Ajai Vir impatiently. "A lot of money. Can you handle it or not?"

She stopped chewing and looked at him.

"Why don't you say what it is then?" she demanded raucously. "Or have you suddenly grown breasts and become shy as a bride?" she resumed chewing.

"Tell this man to leave," demanded Ajai Vir.

She looked at the man indifferently and he walked away.

Ajai Vir leaned forward and spoke softly but firmly. "We want to finish off a man."

She turned her eyes and carefully studied Ajai Vir and then Chris. "You are not CID," she concluded. "How much will you pay?"

"A lot. But he is a big man."

Her lip curled in a sneer and a laugh shook her body. "They are all big men," she said, "except after sex and after the knife slits open their belly." She thought for a moment. "What is his name?"

Ajai Vir hesitated. The die would be cast.

She looked again at him, understanding his hesitation. "We are already lying in one bed," she spat a long stream, wiping her lips with the back of her hand. "Who will now believe that nothing happened? You may as well say something."

"Prabal Kumar," Ajai Vir quickly got it out of his mouth.

She stared emotionlessly into the distance. Ajai Vir couldn't tell if the name meant anything to her. Finally she spoke, "That is a very big name," she admitted.

"Is it too big for you?" demanded Ajai Vir.

"Shall I lift my skirt and show you whether anything is too big for me?" she taunted. Ajai Vir's cheeks flamed, but he checked himself.

169

"Ten lakhs," she said.

Ajai Vir snorted. "Two lakhs."

She held up her forefinger with the thumb on the first index, denoting an inch. "Your thing must be as little as your price," she jeered.

Ajai Vir stood up. "I'll burn you alive," he roared. "My men will burn this brothel to ashes."

She saw she had gone too far. "It is a big man," she mollified, quieter now, "there has to be a big price."

Ajai Vir sat down breathing heavily.

"He's not that big a man," he insisted.

"Unionwallah," she said . " They always have many guards."

Ajai Vir thought. "All right," he barked. "Five lakhs." He raised his hand sharply. "No arguments."

She hesitated, chewing rapidly. "How much advance?"

"None .You will disappear with it."

She stood up at once. "Go home," she said. "This work cannot be done."

"Why do you need it ?" demanded Ajai Vir.

"Are you going to teach me my business?" she howled. "Do I teach you how to screw your wife?"

Ajai Vir sprang to his feet, "Shut up, you whore," he shouted, "I'll have you hung upside down and beaten for a week. I asked you 'why do you need it?' Tell me," he roared.

They glared at each other. Then she turned her face and spat out the wad.

"Somebody will have to be paid off to tell us his programme," her voice was back to its normal, uncouth pitch. "The rest is our job."

"I will give you fifty thousand as advance," barked Ajai Vir "That's all — when will you do it?"

She thought. "Three days," she said flatly. "Some things I like to do quickly." She shook with laughter.

"And if you disappear in the three days?"

"It's not such a big amount," she said indifferently. "These days fifty thousand won't even buy you a Bombay actress," she sneered.

Ajai Vir weighed the options. He decided. He reached inside his jacket and pulled out the Rs.50,000 he had brought. He dropped it at her feet.

"If you disappear," he warned her, "we have many friends in the police. They will find you, and you will regret the day you became a whore."

She bent down, swept up the money and went into her tent.

"Three days," Ajai Vir shouted after her.

He and Chris trudged back.

"Wow," marvelled Chris in the car. "You really fixed that woman. So what's the score?"

"She's going to do it within three days."

"Jeez, I've never seen you like that," wondered Chris. He whistled.

"Aah, it's nothing," Ajai Vir calmed down. "You just have to know how to handle these people. They're either at your feet, or at your throat."

Chris was still wonder-struck, shaking his head at the scene.

"You've got to put some fear into them," explained Ajai Vir, "otherwise they'll just take you for a ride."

"Well. I think you just put the fear of God into her right," admired Chris.

"She'll do it now," said Ajai Vir with quiet confidence. "I just pushed the right buttons. That's all," he nodded grimly.

Three days later, buttons or no buttons, nothing had happened. Ajai Vir waited another two days, then the third morning he set off again for the slum. He seemed disturbed. Chris insisted on coming along.

Behind them, followed two Matador vans full of guards from the factory. All carried five feet long sticks and had clear instructions from Ajai Vir.

"Why don't you tell your Dad?" Chris had asked.

"I'll teach her a lesson on my own," Ajai Vir had replied savagely.

As they turned off the highway, Chris noticed a scooter stalled beside the road and a uniformed policeman tinkering with it.

"Look, there's a cop," pointed out Chris, "want to take him with us?"

Ajai Vir shook his head in fury. "Nothing he can do," he muttered.

The policeman looked up as they passed and Chris noticed he had an open, boyish, sincere face.

They stopped some distance from the place and every one got off, the guards holding their sticks nervously.

"Chris," ordered Ajai Vir, "You stay here. There may be trouble. So don't move from here. Okay?"

Chris nodded. "Sure buddy. Good luck."

The moment they were out of sight, he trailed behind them. They marched quite openly towards the slum lying wrapped in its miasma of smoke and smells. No one was visible. Even the children had disappeared.

All was well till the group passed the first pipe. Then a volley of stones came flying out at them. One hit Ajai Vir on the cheek. As the guards looked around in bewilderment, more rocks thudded into them. Simultaneously, a scooter roared past Chris and the policeman he had noticed earlier screeched to a stop among the group.

"What is happening here?'' he demanded.

The rocks stopped at once. The villagers came out protesting and clamouring pitifully.

"Attackers," alleged one.

"Demons," pleaded another.

"We are very frightened," whimpered a third.

"Please help us," sobbed a woman. "We are poor people."

Some suddenly produced children who on cue began to howl.

The sub-inspector shut off the scooter and pulled it back into its stand. He sat on it and produced a notebook and pen.

"Quiet now," he shouted sternly. "Who are all you people?"

"We are the residents of this area," clamoured the group.

The sub-inspector noted this in his diary.

"And who are you?'' He enquired from Ajai Vir. "And who are these other men and what are they doing here with sticks?"

"They have come here to loot our honour," howled one woman.

The others picked this up instantly.

"For a poor woman," sobbed another, "there is nothing more precious than her honour."

"We may not have money," shouted a man, "but we know how to protect the honour of our womenfolk."

Ajai Vir walked up to the sub-inspector and took him to one side. They had a long conversation and Chris could see the policeman shaking his head, refusing vigorously. Eventually they seemed to have reached an agreement of some sort, because Ajai Vir came stalking back, his handkerchief to his cheek. His troops followed him.

Chris nipped back to the car ahead of them, where the cries of the women fearing for their honour still reached him.

"What happened?" he innocently asked Ajai Vir.

"We'll have to talk to some senior officers," he said grimly.

They were late getting back because Ajai Vir had to go to a nursing home where he received five stiches to sew up his cheek. The moment they reached home, he called a friend who was a senior police officer.

"I've been attacked by a gang of villagers led by this Mirchi woman in the slum behind the cremation ground," Ajai Vir grated. "You have to do something about it, There is a total collapse of law and order in this country."

The officer listened in amazement. "I'll get back to you," he promised noncommittally.

He called back some time later, baffled.

"I say Ajai, what's going on?" he asked. "Sometime ago, a group of villagers from a slum they have named Rajiv Rao Nagar, went to the local police station and claimed that they were singing religious hymns, when you and a gang of men attacked them with sticks. They say they would all have been killed, their women raped and their children carried off into slavery to the Arab countries where you were proposing to sell them to international gamblers who would have tied them to camels and raced them across the desert. Fortunately, they say, a local sub-inspector of the area arrived and at great risk to his own life, saved them. The sub-inspector confirms your presence at the head of a group of armed men."

He resumed. "The complaint was filed by one Gagan Bai, alias Mirchi Madam, who the villagers identify as a devoted social worker of the area. Ms. Bai claims that you became highly enamoured of her and took to visiting her while she was conducting classes on communal harmony, to court her with promises of matrimony. This was in the company of a foreign friend who promised her a Green Card if she eloped with you. When she sternly repulsed your advances, explaining that she has already entered into the holy state of matrimony with one Nathu Ram, alias Nathu Dada, apparently, a local artist held in high esteem, the villagers say, you threatened her with dire consequences. To fulfill your lust and to wreak revenge you descended on them, mercifully, only to be foiled by the gallant sub-inspector who single handedly fought off your entire gang and your own lust-crazed self. The villagers have urged a Bharat Ratna for the sub-inspector." The officer paused. "I say Ajai Vir," he enquired in anxious bewilderment, "have you gone completely nuts or what?"

"Bunch of lies," swore Ajai Vir. "They're all whores."

"Then what the hell were you doing there?"

"Shit," sighed Ajai Vir, "it's a long story. I'll tell you later. But can you hush it up? It's all that Dad needs at this time."

"You should have thought of that before," said the officer. "But I'll see what I can do," he promised. "Meanwhile, why don't you go take a holiday? I think you need some rest."

Ajai Vir took his advise and the same evening left for Goa, leaving instructions with Mr. Sunder on the payment to be made to a sub-inspector who would be turning up.

Chris and Kalpana saw him off at the airport, after which Kalpana drove them to a nearby hotel. The bar was nearly deserted and they settled down and ordered.

Kalpana was disconsolate.

"Chris, this is getting worse and worse."

"Yes," Chris agreed grimly. "You know what happened?"

She nodded. "More or less. Ajai Vir's police friend's wife who is also in the police was a batch-mate of my first cousin in the IAS at Mussoorie."

Chris had long since given up trying to unravel the Gordian knot of Indian relationships but he knew they were widespread, strong and durable.

Kalpana asked, "What was he doing at that slum? You know what the place is, don't you?"

Chris said quickly. "It's not what you think."

She nodded. "He's trying to do something to Prabal Kumar, isn't he?" she asked.

Chris stayed quiet.

"Poor baby," she said softly, "he wants so hard for his Dad to be proud of him. He can't stand to see him go through all this." Her eyes misted. "He has no idea what Indian politics is like . I just hope he hasn't launched any other schemes," she worried. "They'll blow up on him. Its a minefield and he's without a clue. Chris," she asked, "he hasn't done anything else, has he?"

Chris shook his head, He thought about their visit to Bhola and wondered whether to tell her, They paid for their drinks and began to leave, with Chris still hesitating. Eventually he decided not to tell her.

Which was just as well.

Two days later, as Ram Avtar and Chris were having lunch, a group of policemen entered the room. The one leading saluted and said to Ram Avtar. "Please come with us, sir."

Ram Avtar took it calmly. "Am I under arrest?"

"No sir. My orders are only to take you in for questioning."

"On what grounds?"

"Accessory to attempt to murder. Where is your son?"

"Out of town on work."

"We will summon him if necessary. Please come this way."

"Chris," Ram Avtar called out, as he walked out with the policeman. "Phone our lawyers. Ask Sunder for their names. Please request them to be present at the police headquarters."

"Will do," said Chris. "You want me to come too?"

"No, you stay here. Call Kalpana also."

He left, flanked by the policemen.

In the police van he asked. "Who am I supposed to have tried to murder?"

"Prabal Kumar."

Ram Avtar paused. "So that automatically makes me a suspect?"

"Not inevitably, but the attacker has been identified."

"Who is he?"

"A KapCo employee."

Ram Avtar was jolted. "And has he implicated me ?" he asked anxiously.

"He's dead. One of Prabal Kumar's guards shot him."

"And Prabal Kumar himself ?"

"Out of danger. The man attacked him with a crowbar. He aimed for the head, but only got the arm. That's broken, but nothing serious."

At the police headquarters Ram Avtar was greeted politely and taken to a room and asked to sit on a chair. There two police officers took turns questioning him sceptically and relentlessly for hours altogether. Since he genuinely knew nothing, did not know the dead worker either by sight or by name, it rapidly became clear that he was speaking the truth. The clinching evidence was that Lal Verma, who had also been picked up without Ram Avtar being about told it, was being grilled down the same corridor in an identical room.

Both candidly admitted to bribing the workers to return to work. Both began speaking of the meeting with Sevak Chand, but the interrogators hastily changed the subject. Both spoke about the maddening negotiations with the union and every single point they made was exactly the same made by the other . There were no mismatches in their statements.

"But why do you assume I or anyone would need to encourage the worker to attack Prabal? The workers had been beaten in Prabal Kumar's presence, by Prabal Kumar's men. Isn't that motive enough?" asked Ram Avtar.

"What about the worker's family? Why don't you ask them?" suggested Ram Avtar. "Was he angry? Did he feel revengeful? Did anyone meet him to talk to him? Or to incite him? They should have a lot of information."

"He was a bachelor. And a loner," the policeman told him tersely. "His parents and relatives live in Uttar Pradesh. A police party has been despatched to talk to them, But I doubt if he had been in touch with them. I think we have reached a dead end."

Finally they let him go.

"What about my son?" Ram Avtar asked , "You could talk to him too," he offered. "I would like that the whole family should be cleared of suspicion about this attempt."

The interrogator looked at him closely. "Probably not necessary." He hesitated. "Well it can't do any harm, I suppose," he acknowledged. "When would it be convenient for him to drop in for a cup of tea?"

"He's on holiday in Goa. I can recall him whenever you wish," readily accepted Ram Avtar.

"No" concluded the officer. "No need to disturb his holiday. Let me know when he's back and I'll tell you if we need to fix an appointment."

Later, discussing the case with his superior, he asked whether to question Ajai Vir at all.

"May as well" shrugged the superior officer. "What is the harm in it? He's an American educated MBA from a public school background, so he's hardly likely to be involved in murder attempts. But let's have it down on paper that we spoke to him."

"Yes sir," accepted the junior at once. Both knew how important it was to their own careers in the Government of India to have everything conceivable down on paper.

The senior policeman in turn informed his superior, the officer in overall charge of the entire investigation, about the progress on the case.

"The Kapoors are innocent, sir. We are just waiting for the son to return from Goa and we can speak to him as a formality."

The senior officer nodded but said nothing on this. They discussed the other aspects of the case, the shooting of the assailant by Prabal Kumar's guard and whether there were any grounds for suspicion there. This was being closely looked into. They chatted a bit more and the officer reporting saluted and left.

Immediately, the policeman in overall charge made a call on his private line and spoke briefly. Thereafter, the day before Ajai Vir was to return, the officer who had approved his interrogation was transferred to a posting he had long sought and manoeuvred to get. He was delighted, clearing his desk and saying his farewells that same evening. Given the wide publicity the case had got and the political pressure to come to a conclusion, another officer was immediately appointed. He did not think questioning Ajai Vir was of any use at all and said so to the interrogator.

"Let's not waste our time on non-essential people," he said dismissively. "The Commissioner wants results. Bring in all the neighbours at the place the assailant lived and let's find out if any suspicious characters were ever seen visiting him. Let's focus on this angle."

"Yes sir," immediately accepted the interrogator, having also learned how important it was for your career in the Government of India not to contradict your superior.

So Ajai Vir was never questioned at all. And no one of course even thought of speaking to Chris. No one learned of their visit to Bhola Prasad.

14

To celebrate the public exoneration, Ram Avtar decided to throw a party.

"Is it going to be like the farm party?" Chris asked Ajai Vir who had returned looking relaxed and refreshed and apparently permanently cured of any desire to recruit hit men. Or hit women, for that matter.

"No, this'll be older people," said Ajai Vir. "A more sedate and sober crowd."

Chris made a face in disappointment.

Now they circulated among the guests, all of whom were warm in their congratulations to Ram Avtar for having got out of such a perilous situation. He didn't point out that his company was in an even more precarious position but received their good wishes gracefully.

Chis observed with astonishment, the number of middle aged men hugging and fondling each other.

"Are they gay?" he whispered to Kalpana.

"No," she whispered back, "they're Punjabis."

He noticed how when two men spotted each other, they stopped and hurled apparently disgusting obscenities, before charging with whoops at the other, like tectonic plates colliding. He was surprised the earth didn't quake.

Their greetings to their friends' wives were even stranger. They folded their hands, lowered their eyes decorously and cringed with servility. This from men who sent their creditors cheques that bounced with such consistency that you could have played tennis with them. When the wrathful creditors turned up, they didn't turn a hair, charming them instead into an evening at the club where they could all drive down in the Mercedez they had bought with the money saved from sending their creditors bouncing cheques.

But with the women it was all grovelling and '*bhabhi, bhabhi.*'

"What's a 'bhabhi?'" Chris asked Kalpana.

"Brother's wife."

"These guys are all brothers?"

"It's just a figure of speech."

As the party progressed and the drinks flowed, Chris pointed out one or two things to Kalpana, whenever she could find time from playing hostess.

"*Bhabhi*" announced one man, seizing this *Bhabhi* by the waist, "you're looking too cute *yaar*"

The *Bhabhi* tittered and kept a sharp eye out for her husband.

"Sweet," admired Chris. "In America we never regard our friends' wives in this brotherly fashion."

Then he noticed that the man's hand on the *bhabhi*'s back had slipped lower than was strictly brotherly. When it showed no signs of halting its southern decline, Chris was compelled to comment.

"That doesn't look very brotherly."

The *bhabhi* gave the man a sidelong glance.

"You're really such a this thing, *yaar*" she said archly. The man swooned.

"What?" demanded Chris. "What thing?"

Kalpana ordered him to shut up.

"So," the man had recovered his balance, "what have you been doing-shooing?"

"Just kitties, *yaar*" the *bhabhi* responded, having obviously failed to sense the man's hand that had taken up permanent station. "So borial."

"What language are they speaking?" demanded Chris.

"Some excitement-sexcitement there must be?" teased the man.

The *bhabhi*'s narrowed eyes scanned the crowd for her husband, like an AWACS sensing enemy planes. She managed to titter saucily at the same time.

Chris marvelled at her gifts.

"What sex-vex *yaar*" the *bhabhi* prompted, "I'm *tho* only into love-shove."

"Does that mean what I think it does," frantically whispered Chris to Kalpana, who was silently collapsing.

The man preened. "*Voi tho*," he understood completely. "Me too. So let's meet-sheet, *bhabhi*?" he asked.

"*Yaar* you're *tho* so romantic, you're really the limit," she acceded reluctantly to his skilful seduction. "Make a phone-shone tomorrow at 11 in the morning. Let's see," she promised vaguely.

They separated and drifted off in opposite directions, their eyes bright with anticipation.

"Jeez," breathed Chris, "this beats a singles bar."

Kalpana had sped away to look after some newly arrived guests who followed the grand Delhi tradition of reaching when everybody else should be departing.

Chris was passing by his room when he saw that the lights were on inside. Puzzled because he was sure he had turned them off, he opened the door and went in. Aiyar was sitting there on a chair.

"Your two weeks are over," he said with his usual abruptness, "have they agreed?"

183

"How do you get everywhere?" asked Chris. "Were you invited? Are you a friend of the Kapoors?"

Aiyar motioned brusquely. "Have they agreed to change their line of business?"

"It'll kill the old man," protested Chris.

"His new business will bring him back to life," snapped Aiyar.

"And it'll start an entirely new one for you too," he reminded.

The converse, Chris remembered with a shudder, were the aches and the tremblings.

"I need more time," he suggested. "They've got the bank to wait for their payment. It's given them breathing space."

Aiyar shook his head. "Talk to them again tomorrow," he ordered.

"I've tried," explained Chris patiently.

"Tomorrow," Aiyar stood up and walked out. "Tomorrow is another day. And a new life for you."

Chris sighed. He had no objections to making a lot of money, but this guy just didn't understand old man Kapoor.

He turned off the light and went back to the party. It carried on till the early hours of the morning and it was almost dawn before he went to bed.

So he was extremely groggy when he heard the knocking at his door. He checked his watch and saw that it was almost noon. His head felt like a rock band was inside it inventing a hangover blues number.

"Come in," he croaked.

Kalpana walked in, looking shattered.

Chris sat bolt upright. "Is it okay for you to come here alone?" he asked anxiously.

"They've all gone to the Finance Ministry. We're finished."

"That's bullshit. What happened?"

"The bank officially informed us this morning that our request for an extension has been denied. We thought a letter approving it was only a formality. The committee in Bombay had okayed it when we went there. My uncle told me so."

"Then what happened?"

"I called him. He's shocked. He tried speaking to the Chairman, but he's made himself unavailable. My uncle asked around and there are rumours that there were instructions from Delhi. From the Finance Ministry. They've gone to plead their case, but I doubt if it'll help. Chris," she moved up and sat beside him, "you have to help them out,"

"What can I do?"

"Loan them some money. The only way I see out is to pay off Prabal Kumar."

"Jeez, Kalpana, I don't have that kind of dough."

Chris was embarrassed by her intensity and his inability to help.

"They don't need the whole amount. They've got about five crores and they can sell this house and some land they've got and that'll fetch another five crores. Everybody in India knows about the situation in KapCo, so even the loan sharks won't give them any money. You have to help."

"Is Mr. Kapoor ready to pay off Prabal Kumar?" Chris asked.

"I don't know," Kalpana was nearly in tears. "I spoke to Ajai Vir before they left and he feels it's the only way."

Chris was trying to convert rupees into dollars and the unique Indian system of lakhs and crores into the universally accepted hundreds of thousands and millions.

"Dad wouldn't hear of it," he muttered. "But I have a trust fund though I'm not sure how much I could get out of that. I'll have to check. You sure they'll pay me back?"

Kalpana put her head on his chest and howled.

"Hey there," Chris tried to comfort her.

"All of you can always come to America and start a new life. It's a great country. McDonald's is always looking for waitresses."

It didn't seem to help. Still sobbing bitterly she left the room.

Chris got up too and slowly got ready, pondering on the mysteries and tragedies of life. He was sitting in his room trying to figure out how to get the phone number of the lawyer who handled his trust fund without his father finding out.

'I could call Dad's secretary,' he thought, 'but she'd tell Dad right away and he'd want to know what the hell was up. Maybe I can tell him I've found a great investment opportunity and want to put in my own money. But he'd want to know details.'

Chris was pacing up and down still trying to work this out when the Kapoor father and son walked in.

Ram Avtar was looking shrunken and ill, but he was trying to smile and his eyes were moist.

He walked over to Chris and embraced him.

"You are my second son," he said. "Kalpana told me what she had discussed with you and how you agreed and you have given me a new life."

He patted Chris's cheek paternally and with something like love. "You three are my children," he said gently, "and I know you are doing your level best, but this is not the right way."

He stood forlornly in the room and Chris suddenly realised that he was quite a short man.

"Dad, there's no room for ethics in business," Ajai Vir earnestly educated him. "When you're dealing with crooks, let's just pay him off and get on with our lives. Who cares whether it's right or wrong."

Ram Avtar smiled in genuine amusement. He patted Ajai Vir affectionately on his back.

"It's not a question of ethics, my son," he explained softly. "It's just that we have no reason to believe that paying off Prabal Kumar will work."

"But Dad," expostulated Ajai Vir, "once he's got his money, it'll be the last we'll see of him. He'll have got what he wants."

Ram Avtar shook his head, smiling bitterly now. "It may be what he wants," he conceded to Ajai Vir, "but it's not what the politicians want. And Prabal Kumar is only a pawn in their hands. If we pay him off, we will find that we have bankrupted KapCo, bankrupted ourselves and Chris too. I think some very big people are playing for very high stakes with a strong bearing on the nation and its policies. Prabal Kumar will not be allowed to do whatever he pleases. And he knows it too."

He said with certainty. "If we are foolish enough to pay him, he will certainly be smart enough to take it. But nothing will change. After three months if we start to pay less to the workers, what is the guarantee that Prabal will not create another strike? What will we do then?" he asked. "Take him to court for breach of promise? What will we say, that we bribed him? He will merely accuse us of trying to defame him and trying to get out of that mad agreement. What will we do then? We will not even have a roof over our heads or a paisa to call our own. No, my son," he concluded wanly but firmly, "this is not the way. How can we trust a snake that has poisonous teeth on both ends?" he sighed in deep sorrow. "We have just not been able to find a way to make the minister smile," he anguished. "And that has finished us."

"We can't just sit back and wait to be destroyed Dad," said Ajai Vir bitterly. "We must do something."

"Well," reminded Chris, "there's always what I suggested."

Ajai Vir tried to recall, "Can't remember now Chris."

"Start a new business."

"No money Chris," Ajai Vie explained. "And who'd lend it to us?"

"Hell I told you all that would be looked after," said Chris. "Just say the word."

Ram Avtar looked at him sadly but with affection. "Of course if you have a good idea, Chris," he said gently, "that we can always consider. What do you suggest?"

"Well," Chris fumbled, "let me check it out first."

Ram Avtar nodded gently, patted him on his shoulder and he and Ajai Vir left.

Barely a minute later, Chris' phone rang.

"What did he say?" asked Aiyar's voice.

"Jeez," marvelled Chris, "how'd you know they were here?"

"Answer me," snapped Aiyar.

"He said okay," protested Chris. "Don't you ever talk nice?"

He heard Aiyar breathing. His voice unbent. "You have done well," he said. "You will benefit," he promised.

"Great," said Chris, without enthusiasm, "now he wants

to know what new business I have in mind."

"You will be given all the details soon," said Aiyar. "I will instruct you where to come to see me."

He hung up. Slowly Chris put down the receiver. "How does he know everything thats happening?" he puzzled. Hey Christopher, he thought wondering, 'this ain't no place for a football player.'

At that precise moment, a stone came crashing through Christopher's window. The entire pane shattered under the impact and glass tinkled over half the room. Fortunately Chris had been standing besides the wall, so the glass shards flew ahead of him, otherwise he could have been seriously hurt.

Hearing the noise, some servants and guards came running into the room and examined the scene in astonishment. Other people were urgently summoned. Some ran outside to see where the stone could have come from. A shaken Chris was led out and many theories were put forward. Urchins. A disgruntled KapCo employee. Prabal Kumar. God. The policemen outside the wall swore they had seen no one. Within the compound no one had a plausible reason for chucking a stone at Chris. The Kapoors were profusely apologetic but puzzled. The window was rapidly replaced and an armed guard put outside.

Gradually the little crowd disappeared and by the time Chris returned from a lunch everyone tried to keep lively in the dining room, no one else was around.

He noticed a slip of paper lying on his pillow. It said that Mr. Aiyar would see him in exactly half an hour and gave the name and room number of a hotel. Chris left immediately.

He took a taxi to the hotel, which was a small one tucked inside a lane of an unobtrusive South Delhi colony. He walked in and the receptionist diligently kept his face lowered. Chris took the stairs to the first floor, went down a discreetly lit corridor with dark blue carpeting and found the room he wanted.

He opened the door, went in, shut the door behind him and stopped speechless.

In front of him was the mysterious Latin American he had kept glimpsing. He was sprawled on a sofa, with a nearly empty bottle of Indian whisky in front of him. He was obviously very drunk. He waved a glass whose contents splashed about liberally.

"Sit down Chris," he said pointing to a chair, "We're old friends now." He laughed slightly hysterically.

Carefully, Chris lowered himself, his mind refusing to function. 'This,' he finally told himself, 'beats everything I've ever seen.'

The South American poured him a drink and handed over the glass. Chris noticed that he was sweating heavily like the first few times he had seen him. The man's hands were trembling and his face twitched.

He raised his glass. "To life," he toasted. "To its twists and turns and traps. Here's to you Chris."

Chris raised his glass politely. "Guess you have the better of me. I don't know what you're talking about. In fact I don't even know your name."

"My name?" The man examined this question with astonishment. "Yes, truly, I often forget myself what is my name?" He pondered this mystery. Finally, he decided, "Just call me Baretta." He exploded with laughter.

Chris failed to see the joke. "Thats not your real name?" he asked.

"No more than Mian Shankar Aiyar."

Once again Chris was paralysed. Baretta, or whatever his name was, got up swaying. "A minute, Chris," he excused himself. "Too much booze. Back in a minute and then we'll talk."

He lurched off to the bathroom.

"Yeah," said Chris after him, "we gotta talk. And how."

15

Baretta returned a few minutes later. He had wiped his face and was swaying less than earlier, but he still looked ashen and trembled sporadically. He opened a new bottle of whisky, set it down on the table in front of the sofa and sat back.

"So what's up?" immediately questioned Chris. "Who are you? What do you want with me?"

Baretta sat thinking and drinking, obviously trying to frame an answer.

"Okay," said Chris. "Are you selling drugs?"

Baretta laughed again, the sound ending in a whimper.

'Jeez,' thought Chris in sympathy, 'this guy's gone to pieces.'

"All right Mr. Baretta," Chris said kindly. "Is this some kind of weird ghost stuff? You know, like things from beyond the grave kind of crap. Some really spooky stuff has been happening. Do you need a priest or something like in *The Exorcist*?"

Baretta finally spoke. "We may both need divine aid. I think we're both damned."

"So it is spooky stuff?" asked Chris, incredulous, but given the events of the past, a bit unsure. "Like that TV show *Beyond The Twilight Zone*?"

Baretta shook his head, drank deep and sighed.

"What is it?" urged Chris. "Come on. What is it? It's killing you too."

Baretta winced at the word 'killing' and sighed again.

192

He held his glass in both hands and looked despairingly in it. His face was twitching again.

"I am sworn never to reveal this," he said. "I'm breaking the most solemn promise a man can make. But you see," he looked pleadingly at Chris, asking for his understanding. "I have two daughters. After my wife's death, there's no one to bring them up. Lovely girls." His face softened. "But I need a few more years till they can look after themselves. After that," he shrugged, drinking again, "I don't really care what happens to me. But I need a few more years," he begged.

Chris waited for him to continue. He didn't, his eyes still imploringly on Chris. "Okay, you got them. What am I supposed to do about it?" Chris demanded plaintively.

"Don't let Kapoor change his line of business," begged Baretta.

Chris leaned back. Then he slowly put his glass in front of him and stood up. "Hey buddy," he said in farewell, "I'm out of here."

"No, no, no," waved Baretta in alarm. "It's dangerous for you too."

"Look," said Chris in exasperation. "Either you talk straight, I'm heading for the hills danger or not."

Baretta sighed again and clutched his glass. His face was dripping again.

"All right," he conceded in a small voice. "Sit down. I'll talk."

Chris sat, but on the edge of the chair, ready to rise and leave if there was any more nonsense from this pitiful, drunken wreck.

"All right," Chris said firmly. "I've had just about enough of this mumbo-jumbo stuff. Now I'm asking you for the last time. What's going on?"

Baretta looked at him again with tragic, tormented eyes.

"You have aroused the interest of certain intelligence agencies," he finally said with difficulty.

Chris considered this. "What the hell for?" he asked.

"It's a long story," said Baretta.

"Hey," said Chris toughly, "are you talking, or am I going?"

The man raised a hand to placate him. "Since I've told you this much," he said wearily, "I may as well tell you the rest."

"Now you're talkin'" encouraged Chris. "Don't stop. Which intelligence agency? The CIA?"

Baretta shook his head, now obviously anxious to get it all off his chest.

"No," he said, "Pakistani intelligence."

Chris was astonished. "And they can do all this funny stuff? I thought the only thing they were good at was peddling drugs."

Baretta nodded. "Yes they can. All intelligence agencies can."

"And who's Aiyar?"

"He's a Pakistani Intelligence Officer."

"Not with a name like Aiyar," contradicted Chris, "I asked someone and it's an Indian name."

"It's a cover name" explained Baretta. "If you go complaining, it'll mean nothing. Not about where the guy's from, or which religion, or even whether he's pretending to be a prominent Indian personality. Complete confusion."

"Jeez," said Chris, "that's all I need. What if the cops back home find out?"

"No, no," Baretta reassured him. "No one will know.

This is an intelligence agency so secret that even the Pakistani Government has forgotten about its existence."

"How'd that happen?"

Baretta sighed. "Sometimes mistakes occur in the intelligence business," he admitted. "This agency which calls itself the Hindustan Fan Club, or HFC, was set up by a senior Pakistani official. After it came into existence, the HFC decided that their creator knew too much about them and in order to maintain total secrecy, they eliminated him. Unfortunately," he condoled, "they found they had been a bit premature."

"How come?"

"They discovered the senior official hadn't got around to telling anybody else about the Hindustan Fan Club. So they didn't know who to talk to in the Pakistani Government and indeed who could be trusted. The only man who knew a bit was the senior official's typist, to whom he had begun dictating the note about the HFC at the time of his unfortunate demise. So they terminated him too."

"Sounds dangerous," said Chris with a shudder.

"They're deadly," agreed Baretta. "And totally dedicated. Why, they are ready to lay down the life of the last Pakistani politician in their cause."

"Wow," admired Chris at such commitment. "But if their own Government doesn't know about them, who pays their salaries?"

Baretta acknowledged the point. "They sell cricket bats," he said. "Before the Pakistani official's demise, he had ordered them to open a chain of stores specialising in selling cricket bats all over India as a cover for their activities. This HFC did with such success, that on their creator's death they found they didn't really need any outside funding for themselves and their operations. So they thought why inform their Government and go through the nuisance of filing reports and risking a leak that would jeopardise their lives? They decided to just continue on their own and stay self-sufficient."

"Not bad," admired Chris. "Have they achieved anything here?"

"A lot," said Baretta. "In fact, quite a lot. They were the first to find out about a great many things the Indians were up to much before anyone else in the world."

"Well," grinned Chris in malice, thinking of Sevak Chand, "the Indian Government couldn't have had much to smile about after that."

Baretta shook his head sadly. "Unfortunately," he admitted, "there was a slight problem. You see," he lamented, "they couldn't tell anyone in the Pakistani Government what they had found out without revealing their own existence, which might have been leaked to the Indians. This could have been fatal, since the Indians are completely ruthless bastards. So they didn't tell anyone. But they knew," he said nodding his head in appreciation. "They really knew and it was a great consolation."

"Well," asked Chris, "what do they want from me?"

"They want you to set up a similar chain of stores selling cricket bats all over the United States."

"Jeez," expostulated Chris, "what the hell for? Nobody plays cricket in the USA. Whats the use of these stores?"

Baretta nodded significantly. Clearly he had great regard for the HFC. "Nobody knows why," he said smiling cunningly.

"Ah," Chris understood, "you mean nobody except the Hindustan Fan Club?"

"No" explained Baretta patiently. "They don't know why either."

"What?" asked Chris befuddled. "Then who does?"

"Nobody," repeated Bretta. "That's the genius of it, don't you see? Their strategy is that if they even don't know why they're doing something, then how can anyone else? Ultimate security," he marvelled.

Chris tried to digest this. "And what do they want KapCo to do?"

"They want them to make the cricket bats that'll be sold by you."

"They'll go broke," protested Chris. "Nobody'll buy no damn cricket bats in the USA. Why are they after the Kapoors, for Chrissake?" he asked angrily. "They're in enough trouble already with their government."

"That's why," agreed Baretta. "They'll be so angry with their Government, that they're likely to do anything HFC asks."

"Yup," Chris saw the logic of this. "That makes some sense at least."

Baretta gestured with his hands. "That's the intelligence business," he said, "a little bit of sense. A whole lot of nonsense."

He drank again from his glass and seemed to be feeling better.

"In fact," he added, "HFC has done a lot to worsen the Kapoor's problems so that they would be ripe for the plucking."

"Yup," agreed Chris again. "They've had a whole bunch of bad luck."

Baretta smiled wisely. "Anytime anybody has too much good luck or too much bad luck," he tittered, "it's not luck. It's an intelligence agency."

"But people also kept trying to stop me from getting old man Kapoor to change his business," remembered Chris. "All that Faustus stuff. Who was that?"

"That," Baretta drank long and deep from his glass, obviously fortifying himself for greater revelations, "were the people who are trying to stop the Pakistanis."

"Oh," said Chris, "who's that?"

"The Aruba Secret Service."

"Aruba?" said Chris incredulously. "Knew a girl from there that went out with a buddy of mine. Why the hell would Aruba be interested?"

"Because they are the largest suppliers of baseball bats to the United States and they don't want competition from any chain of cricket bat stores."

"Horseshit," derided Chris. "There'll never be any competition. It's something else, isn't it?" He looked keenly at Baretta.

The South American acknowledged Chris' perspicacity.

"Yes," he admitted. "There is another reason." He hesitated.

"Come on," demanded Chris. "Out with it. What?"

"Aruba wants to destroy HFC's chain of cricket bat stores in India."

"Why? They're no competition to Aruba?"

"If cricket bats disappear from the Indian market," explained Baretta, "then Aruba stands a better chance."

"Chance of what?"

"Of selling baseball bats to India."

"Oh mother," Chris groaned. "Nobody plays baseball in India. Why doesn't somebody tell the Aruba Government that?"

Baretta shrugged. "The Indian cops could always use them. They've got these stupid sticks right now. Anyway," his voice rose threateningly, "intelligence agencies don't make policies, they just follow orders. Besides, if 900 million Indians bought baseball bats from Aruba, think, it would transform our economy. So my orders are explicit... at all costs, stop Kapoor from changing his line of business."

Chris let him subside.

"Okay," Chris conceded soothingly. "They do what they're told to do. But who the hell are you?" He asked with very real wonder "and why are you telling me all this?"

Baretta's hand which had steadied somewhat began to tremble again as he remembered something. His face began to twitch rapidly. He refilled his glass breathing noisily.

"All right," soothed Chris, recognising an imminent nervous collapse.

"We'll leave it be for now. But tell me," he asked, "how did I get all those belly aches and goose bumps and stuff at all those times?"

Baretta leaned back, on less shaky ground now.

"Timed toxins," he explained. "Every molecule of the human body and mind can have anything done to it, for as long as is needed, for whatever length of time, whenever," he boasted. "Any disease, any illness, any disorder, physical or mental or of the bone, it can all be arranged."

"How?" Chris was amazed.

"Liquids, powders, gases," Baretta shrugged. "Its easy."

"What do they do it for?"

"It weakens the will to resist."

"Charming," grunted Chris. "And all those signs I kept seeing about Aiyars? What was that all about?"

"Psychological warfare," explained Baretta. "Your

199

psychological profile would have been drawn up by an expert and the people controlling the operation would know exactly how to manipulate you and how far to push."

"Push me for what?"

"Keep you under stress. A mixture of toxins and tension brings people quite rapidly to heel. And of course carrots."

"Carrots," snorted Chris, "hate the stuff. I'm a steak man."

Baretta giggled. "Not literally," he explained. "Inducements."

Chris recalled. "Like the millions I was supposed to make from the stores in the USA?"

"Right. You take a bite of the carrot, its pulled away and you have to jump higher the next time for the next bite."

"But what's the purpose of all this?" It was Chris' turn to plead.

"Control," explained Baretta. "Above all else, an intelligence officer needs absolute, total and unquestioning obedience from his agents. You see," he elaborated, "it's like if you're playing a game of chess. Understand?"

Chris nodded.

"So," Baretta continued, "only you know the overall plan, which your opponent has to try and figure out. You have various pieces in front of you, each capable of certain powers. When you move a pawn, you have to be damn sure it does what you want it to do and just that. Nothing more, nothing less. It would be impossible for you to play the game if the pawn decided to move four steps instead of the one you want. Okay? That's why the intelligence officer needs total control."

"Well if they wanted me to do something, why didn't

they ask nicely? Why was Aiyar so damn rude about it?" complained Chris.

"The promise of rewards, coupled with toxins and harshness, verbal, or physical, or psychological, usually breaks people down into total obedience."

"But look" Chris confessed, "I'm no chess player. Hell, I'm just a plain, ordinary football jock. Us jocks are pretty dumb. Let's face it, what good would I be in a chess fight?"

"You're not the chess player," sighed Baretta, "the intelligence officer is. You're just the pawn. And a dumb jock is exactly what the intelligence officer needs. He doesn't want somebody who'll figure out what his end game plan is, or do more than he's told to, or be so bright as to become a double agent. He wants a creature who will do exactly what he's told to do. You're perfect."

Chris puzzled over this. "And these guys are not worried that I might complain to the cops? I mean poisons and this psychological stuff can't be legal, can it?"

"It's not. But how would you prove it?" asked Baretta. "The toxins are undetectable by even the most sensitive instruments and if you complained about the psychological warfare, you would appear to have symptoms indistinguishable from schizophrenic paranoia. You'd be hospitalised, sent to a lunatic asylum."

"Well," erupted Chris, "they've forgotten one li'l ol' thing. I'm a citizen of the United States of America and buddy, let me tell you, we're the world's only superpower. Now I'm telling you, back where I come from, my family packs a lot of clout. I think you better warn these guys..." he trailed off as Baretta shook his head sorrowfully.

"Nobody will help you," he explained gently. "Once you agree to work for an intelligence agency, you belong to them body and soul and for good. Remember Faustus. Even your own mighty nation will not come to your help."

Chris was horrified. "And all this just to sell cricket bats?" he asked incredulously.

"We do the most diabolical things for the most trivial reasons," accepted Baretta.

"Sounds like they're all nuts to me," expostulated Chris, "Jeez, can't they find an easier way to make a living? This is really rotten."

Baretta's eyes shone with outrage. "Never forget," he snapped, "that no one is quicker to take offence than an intelligence officer. We can teach you a life long lesson and not leave a mark..." He calmed down. "Its not that all intelligence officers are delighted with the way things are," he explained. "Many are sickened by what they have to do to people who don't even know they've done anything wrong."

"Why don't the officers tell them to quit it?" asked Chris.

"No. Once someone has been recruited, no other intelligence agency speaks to him directly, other than through signals. If he has any sense, he picks them up."

He forestalled Chris' protest. "That's the way the game is played all over the world."

"And Governments allow this?"

"Yes. Any country is free to try and recruit anyone else, particularly in the democracies. Which is fine if the people recruited believe in what they're doing. But they should realise there's no going back and no one beside their recruiter to turn to."

"Shit," breathed Chris. "Who elected these guys to make all these rules? I never voted for nothing like this I can tell you."

Baretta smiled cynically. "The world isn't run according to the way people vote."

Something was nudging Chris' mind.

"We," he finally remembered. "You said 'we' were talking about intelligence officers. You're one," he said with conviction. "Who are you?"

Baretta nodded sloppily in agreement. By now he was so drunk that he probably didn't care what he said.

"I am the New Delhi Station Chief of the Aruba Secret Service," he said simply.

Chris didn't know how to react. "And you kept trying to warn me through your signals and stuff not to let Mr. Kapoor change his business."

Baretta nodded. "Yes."

"How'd you know so much about what the Hindustan Fan Club is up to if even their own damn government doesn't know they exist?"

"After Aruba took a decision to try and sell baseball bats to India, we closely looked at all the cricket suppliers and stumbled onto HFC. Since then we've had them under intense and complete 24 hours surveillance. Room bugs, phone taps, hidden fibre optic cameras, trailing people, the works."

"Well," said Chris, "too bad. You'll just have to tell your Government that you've failed. He's changing his line of business. Though I doubt if he's going to make cricket bats for the US market," he said sardonically. "He'll just have to think of something else. You'll have to tell your government that you've failed."

Suddenly tears rose in Baretta's eyes and came coursing down his cheeks.

Chris was shaken. "There," he handed his handkerchief to the man, a soft touch as always, though admittedly, it is a heart-rending sight to see a master spy weep. "Hey, its okay. Jeez, they won't kill you for failing. Cheer up."

Baretta wept even harder. "My poor daughters," he said, "Orphaned."

"That's rubbish now," Chris jollied him up, "they'll just give you another assignment."

Baretta shook his head in despair. "It's worse than that," he sobbed, "You see, Kapoor is not going to change his line of work."

Chris laughed reassuringly at that. "Hey pal, take my word for it. He is."

"No, no," howled Baretta in agony, "he's not, believe me. The Aruba Secret Service has the Government of India completely penetrated. I should know. Ram Avtar Kapoor has found a way to make the minister smile. Right now he is in a private meeting with Sevak Chand. After this he will never change his line of work."

"First time I've heard of it," said Chris, "But hey, what're you howling about? It's perfect for you. You can claim you stopped him from changing his line of business. You'll be a hero. Hell," he slapped him on the shoulder, "they'll honour you with the Royal Order of the Smallest Bikini, or whatever the hell award Aruba has. Brighten up buddy."

Baretta slowly slid off the sofa onto the carpet where his weeping increased. "I was lying," he sobbed. "For the sake of my daughters," he implored Chris, "make Kapoor change his business."

Chris grabbed Baretta's glass and drank it in a gulp. He strode to the bathroom and washed his face. He returned wiping it with a towel, took several deep breaths and helped Baretta to sit again on the sofa.

204

"There now," he said gently, "feel better. Here, have some water."

As Baretta gulped down the bottle of mineral water, Chris wondered whether he had lost his mind, or Baretta had, or perhaps both.

"Now," he said with all the gentleness he could muster, "tell papa Christopher all. Were you making it all up?"

"No, no," protested Baretta, still blubbering. "Every word I've told you is true. It's just that I do want Ram Avtar to change his business."

Chris felt himself grow dizzy. He let go of Baretta who he had been helping stay erect and abandoning his pose of kindliness, slumped down in a chair.

"What the fuck, man?" he pleaded. "What gives?"

Baretta's sobs ended though he still whimpered occasionally... He started his story.

"Once," he said, "I was the brightest rising star of the Aruba Secret Service. I was so proud," he recalled, sniffling still, "I was the most promising officer of the greatest intelligence agency of the greatest nation on earth."

Chris let it pass.

"So trusted was I, that when rival intelligence agencies tried to recruit me, I reported it at once to my superiors and under their orders and their control, I became a double agent, supposedly working for these other countries, but actually serving my own beloved Aruba. Under the orders of my actual masters in Aruba, I passed on a stream of disinformation to these countries and successfully executed numerous intricate and delicate operations to penetrate them in return, to identify potential agents in their midst and to recruit them to the cause of Aruba. I never failed."

He sniffed miserably and blew his nose. He resumed.

"Bit by bit I began to notice a change in my superiors. But it was too late to correct the error of my ways. You see," his eyes watered as he looked pitifully at Chris, "I was too successful. Since I never failed, my bosses began to suspect it was because I was actually working for these foreign agencies rather than for Aruba and my own brilliantly executed operations were accomplished with the help of these agencies to build up my credibility with my own people, so I could be promoted to more senior positions. This suspicion became a conviction and I have been sent to India as a last chance. If I succeed in this manifestly mad attempt, my masters will have no further doubts that I am working for several foreign powers, perhaps some I have not even told them about. And the consequences would be of the utmost severity for me. Therefore," he begged Chris, tears springing up again, "for the sake of my life, for the sake of my two little daughters, I must fail. Please," he begged, "Ram Avtar must start making baseball bats. My life depends on it."

Chris got up exhaustedly. "Look," he pacified, "none of this makes no sense to me. Lemme think about it and I'll get back to you. Okay? How does that sound? Besides," he added, "'I've got to figure out what to do about this Pakistani guy. Nobody but nobody owns me, that's for sure."

"You can talk," bitterly complained Baretta, "your problems are over, he's gone,"

"Gone?" asked Chris," where to"

"He too had come under suspicion from his superiors."

"What about?"

"He was accused anonymously of having a conscience and was therefore under watch by his own people. It was a serious accusation but of course HFC would never act without decisive and unquestionable proof."

"So what happened?"

"When he gave you two weeks to get Kapoor to agree to change his line of business, it became clear that the problem was certain and beyond redemption. He has therefore been terminated by HFC."

Chris couldn't absorb any of this.

"Well, got to go," he headed out . "Great talking to you. Check you out later."

Behind him Baretta sat with his hands squeezed between his knees, the picture of woe. He didn't even look at Chris leave. Tears dripped onto the carpet. He did not look like much of a master spy at all.

16

Chris arrived at the Kapoor residence and as he went in, he was accosted by Mr.. Sunder who looked at him slyly.

"All fine sir," he said bashfully. "All well sir."

Chris was astonished. "You mean Mr. Kapoor's swung it?"

Mr. Sunder began to look wary, remembering his last conversation with Chris. His voice lowered to a whisper.

"I mean the socially relevant magazines sir," he hissed. "They've arrived."

"Oh the *Playboys*" exclaimed Chris, causing Mr. Sunder to hastily look around. "Hey great. I asked for some from back home for your friends. Now they can see what America's really like. Hope they find it educational."

"Thank you sir," Mr. Sunder bowed humbly and began to retreat.

"Hey buddy," Chris reassured him, "anything to help the cause of education."

Mr. Sunder disappeared into his domain and Chris strode on. 'Left to Mr. Sunder' he mused, 'he'd make Hugh Hefner President of Delhi University.'

He met Ajai Vir coming out of the house.

"So how's it going?" He asked not wanting to reveal that he knew about Ram Avtar's meeting with Sevak Chand.

Ajai Vir shrugged.

"Don't know. Dad says he's come to a decision. Now he's in his room, praying."

"So his meeting was good with the minister? Sevak Chand smiled or what?"

Ajai Vir looked puzzled.

"What meeting?" he asked. "Dad went out to see one of our lawyers, he said. He's just come back. He's asked me to call a press conference urgently for tomorrow night and he's going to announce what he's decided."

Chris stayed quiet, not sure whether Baretta had been wrong or if Ram Avtar hadn't told Ajay Vir.

He didn't get to speak to Ram Avtar after that since he was constantly out of the house. Ajay Vir too was away all the time, personally visiting newspaper offices to invite them for the conference.

They had managed to hire the rooftop hall at the Taj Hotel despite the short notice and much to everyone's surprise, it was packed with reporters even before the appointed time.

Chris sat in the corner in the front row and while waiting for the proceedings to begin, looked down at the lights of New Delhi. There was winter mist that wreathed itself around everything and through which the lights glowed.

He suddenly remembered a German girl he had dated briefly. She had been an exchange student and often bewildered by America, she would exclaim in German. 'Nicht Und Nacht.'

"What's that mean?" he had asked her.

"Night and fog. I am, how you say, lost."

Now he thought again of the saying and how appropriate it was to this city even in the daytime and under a bright sun. But now at night, wrapped in a mist through which you sensed rather than saw movement, he felt particularly lost.

He started as he heard Lal Verma's voice from the row

209

of chairs behind a wooden table that had been set to face the audience. Besides Verma sat Ram Avtar, then Ajai Vir and after that two other managers of KapCo who had been roped in to fill the remaining chairs.

Verma welcomed everyone, briefly reminded them of the history of the strike, the violence and then the list of demands made by the union led by Prabal Kumar, including the one about taxi fare for each worker, one in each air conditioned and imported taxi, from the highway to the factory, via the Badhkal bar.

"We have given deep thought to all the demands and based upon what we feel is fair and just, both to the workers and to KapCo and according to the wage structure that is prevalent all over India, we have come to a decision. I now invite our Chairman and Managing Director, Shri Ram Avtar Kapoor to address you."

Ram Avtar switched on the microphone in front of him and spoke briefly.

"The wage structure of the workers is at par with those of other companies everywhere," he said. "Many of our workmen started with us when I started the company, or are the second generation of a family working with us. It would not be ethical to have an underpaid workforce, nor would it be good business sense. Yet," he paused to sip water from a glass, "it would be impossible to agree to the demands made by the Prabal Kumar - led union, without making KapCo completely uncompetitive. In fact, without bankrupting ourselves. Nonetheless, given that our workers seem," he paused here searching for the right word and it suddenly occurred to Chris that the level of Ram Avtar's English varied according to the audience he was addressing, "our workers seem homesick for more." He stopped as a rumble of laughter rolled

210

through the journalists. "Given that our workers seem homesick for more, we are prepared to offer a 25 per cent increase to all workers in their basic wage, as well as a further 25 per cent linked to performance. We believe this is not just fair, but generous." He stopped abruptly. "I invite questions now."

Nearly every hand went up and he pointed to a venerable gentleman who he noticed had been among the first to arrive, who had seated himself in the first row and had been profusely taking notes.

The journalist rose to his feet shakily.

"I feel..." he wheezed in a piercing though unsteady voice.

Lal Verma interrupted him.

"Please introduce yourself sir."

The man looked baffled. The other journalists prompted him. "Name and paper," they hissed.

His brow cleared. "Kumar from the *Faizabad Gambhir Samasya*," he announced. He cleared his throat and shut his eyes in concentration as he reformulated his thoughts.

"I feel," he resumed, "that India's dismal performance, I would even say disgusting performance in the field of sports is due to the cheap vulgarity, I would even say pornography, being depicted in Hindi films. Young girls are being shown almost naked and the cheap movements you cannot even imagine. This is completely against the spirit of our glorious culture that has withstood the test of time. In fact if you were to closely watch some of these so called Hindi films with their heroines in tight tight dresses, you will imagine that you are not in India but in Sweden or Mar ." He sat down.

There was considerable consternation among the KapCo executives who consulted urgently among themselves. Finally Lal Verma was elected to speak.

"What is your question sir?" he asked cautiously, not certain if this was some cunning journalistic device to entrap them.

Kumar rose even more unsteadily to his feet, this time in rage.

"Who you are to question me?" he thundered. "The country is full of naked naked girls and you are questioning me! Do you know that I have personally asked questions to Jawaharlal Nehru on his policies at press conferences and now you are questioning me?" He seemed prepared to continue.

Other journalistic voices rose. "Oi Kumar, shut up."

"Give him a drink," suggested another.

"Make it a bottle," warned a third.

A kind though firm hand seized Kumar's collar from behind and dragged him back to his chair where he sat muttering about naked naked girls.

The other questions were less unorthodox and Ram Avtar handled them with ease. 'No, he was not going to negotiate. This was his final offer. No, he had not spoken to Prabal Kumar, this is all that he had to say, Thank you gentlemen. The bar is now open.'

This was followed by the customary sprint in the direction of the drinks and Chris wondered if India's quest for an athletic gold in the Olympics would be finally fulfilled if whisky bottles were placed at the finishing line and some of Delhi's more legendary press conference attendees invited to do their bit for the country. He thought it might work if other countries didn't send some of their own press people.

The next day the newspapers were full of the KapCo decision and there was much speculation about what Prabal Kumar would do now. All the papers agreed that this was

212

the crucial test of his credibility. Prabal Kumar sensed this too and arrived at the factory gates to exhort the workers to hold firm. In a stinging rejoinder to Ram Avtar's offer, he characterised it as "charity to a beggar. We are not beggars," he thundered, "we are partners. We are the real owners."

He made one of his longest and fieriest speeches ever, but at the end the workers responded disspiritedly, even though his assistants shouted themselves hoarse trying to whip up their enthusiasm.

Prabal Kumar left in deep thought and an hour later his own men, again equipped with sticks and iron rods arrived in a van and positioned themselves inconspicuously where they could watch the workers. However, they did make sure the workers were aware of their presence.

Meanwhile, another group of workers held a rally in Delhi, agreeing to the terms offered and demanding that they be allowed to resume work. Prabal Kumar denounced them in the strongest terms and alleged that they had been bribed by the management.

This group arrived at the factory and parked themselves at the other side of the highway, though they made no move to enter the factory. Ram Avtar ordered that the factory gates be opened and kept opened day and night, so that whichever worker wanted to resume work, could go in. When a reporter called to question him, he agreed that it was merely symbolic but said that he felt it was necessary that the workers feel that the factory was their home and that they were always welcome there. He described the strike as "a family dispute and which family is there which doesn't have quarrels" he asked. In fact, he added with a chuckle, "It is these little quarrels that make us value each other more." He ended by appealing to the workers to reunite the KapCo family and make it happy and prosperous again.

Alarmed by this, the Government sent armed police to the site and announced that they had been ordered to use whatever measures were necessary to prevent bloodshed. By this it was presumed that what the Government meant was that it was okay for the cops to create bloodshed among the workers, but not for the workers to create bloodshed among the other workers.

Prabal Kumar hastily swore that there would be no violence and in a brief though moving ceremony at Rajghat, announced that the only path acceptable in a democracy was the one shown by Bapu and anything else was to be condemned. He had a *tilak* applied to his forehead from the soil nearby which he said was sacred because Bapu had walked there.

It was not immediately clear how the Father of the Nation had walked to the spot where his ashes were meant to be buried, but the Government was apparently impressed enough not to arrest Prabal.

A few days later, at dawn, the workers who wanted to end the strike and who numbered about a hundred and fifty, in an obviously pre-determined move, raced across the deserted highway and before Prabal Kumar's stunned men could react, had entered the factory. There they produced chains they had tied around their bodies and chained themselves by their legs to the machines and padlocked. The keys were taken away by one of their numbers and in full view of the public and press ceremoniously thrown from a bridge into the Yamuna. They announced to the journalists that they would allow their chains to be sawed away once they were assured that they could resume work.

Prabal Kumar stood outside the factory all day, exhorting them through a loud speaker to come out, promising them an infinitely better package than the one offered by Ram Avtar, even pleading with them not to be misled by the management who were devils personified.

The police waited with guns ready, but no violence occurred. Prabal Kumar made no effort to storm the factory and towards evening they relaxed when he left.

The workers chained to their machines cheered when they heard he had returned to Delhi for the night. They ate with a special relish the food the guards brought for them under Lal Verma's instructions, and joked delightedly among themselves before lying down on the floor to sleep. The chains restricted their movements but they were able to doze.

No one still knows exactly how it happened and in fact the committee set up by the government to investigate the mystery is still minutely examining the whole issue. What is known is that a little past midnight, a fire broke out in the factory. Whether it was sabotage or a short circuit is still to be uncovered by the committee, but the fire spread rapidly.

After the strike had started, a lot of the raw material had been left unused and uncollected around the machines. This ignited with the heat and the entire building began to burn with intensity.

The guards and the striking workers outside came running in when they heard the screams of the men, saw the red rage of the fire and smelt the stinging smoke. But they were helpless in trying to break the chains tying the workers to their machines. Strain as they might, not one link snapped and soon they had to flee to escape the fire ball that came licking like a monsoon of red.

Someone ran and called the policemen and begged them

to use their rifles to shoot away the locks and the policemen shambled back to their tents to get their guns. But by the time they returned, the entire building was a furnace and they were driven away by the searing heat.

Everyone milled around helplessly, listening to the shrieks of the helpless workers chained to their machines being roasted alive. The air was heavy with the odour of burning flesh. The fire engines arrived but it was too late and their number too few. All the workers inside died as well as three guards who had waited too long and been overcome by the smoke. Totally a hundred and fifty two people died in the inferno

The next day was one the Government would like to forget. The opposition parties, the press, the industry bodies, turned as one upon the Government. Public opinion was horrified.

The BJP demanded the resignation of the government. The CPM staged violent rallies calling for the rolling back of the liberalisation programme. "This is just the first episode," warned one leader. "All of India will lie in ashes by the time the multinational companies are through."

The industry apex associations pointed out the dangers inherent in allowing "irresponsible and violent trade union activities that inexorably lead to tragedy." They appealed for a partnership between the industry and government to forestall such happenings in the future. Foreign investors began to express apprehensions at the suitability of India as a safe destination for their funds. The major newspapers expressed horror and an editorial announced its belief that the Congress had forfeited the right to govern and asked for a new election.

After a full 24 hours of what appeared to be dithering, but were actually being used for urgent conferences where all possibilities were considered and their implications evaluated, the Government began to move.

Prabal Kumar was arrested under a section of the law that did not give him the right to get bail. His associates, who were widely suspected to have caused the fire, were also taken into custody for questioning. An unnamed government official grimly informed reporters "that the suspects will talk. Have no doubts on that." This caused great pleasure among the public. A retired judge was appointed to investigate the entire tragedy with clear, stern and explicit instructions that he deliver his findings "with all possible speed, bearing in mind of course the need for a full and thorough enquiry that fulfils the need for truth, objectivity and the ends of natural justice." He was assured of all assistance in the matter of funds and personnel as soon as the necessary paper work was completed.

The Prime Minister himself in a statement regretted the tragedy but felt that the soul of liberalisation was not affected. Indian's foreign missions were instructed to meet potential investors to assure them that it was not customary for Indian workers to be burned alive by the dozen and this was an exceptional case. In answer to a specific query, an Ambassador assured the concerned questioner that he would not be normally expected to set fire to his workers. A Pakistani allegation in the United Nations that most of the dead workers were Kashmiris led to an unholy row, the cancellation of the visit by a water polo team and a further setback to bilateral relations.

In Punjabi Bagh Ajai Vir and Chris sat in Ram Avtar's bedroom, shocked and haggard Ram Avtar, who had shaved and showered, sat cross legged in front of his wife's picture, tinkling the little bell. The small lamp burned fitfully. He mumbled his prayers and in between occasionally answered in monosyllables to the questions put by the young men.

"Does this mean we're finished, Dad?" asked Ajai Vir.

Ram Avtar said nothing, his prayers continuing.

"But we're dead Dad," insisted Ajai Vir. "Who'll come and work for us now?"

Ram Avtar still mumbled his prayers.

"And even if they do agree," Ajai Vir anguished, "how will we rebuild the factory? Its in ashes."

Ram Avtar bowed. "Insurance," he said briefly.

"The whole thing?' Chris asked incredulously.

Ram Avtar nodded, mumbling his prayer.

"But it'll be years before we start again," Ajai protested. "We'll be forgotten by then."

Ram Avtar turned the page of the scripture in front of him. "Six months," he said and the volume of his prayers increased.

"But people won't spit on our products," Ajai Vir protested. "We'll have lost all our goodwill."

Ram Avtar gestured in irritation for them to leave. He looked up quickly once in the middle of the prayer and said, "We're the victims. Everything will be fine," and resumed his mumblings.

The duo slowly wound their way out. Ram Avtar scattered the auspicious rice on the framed picture of his wife. His eyes gleamed as he looked at her. 'We've won,' he communicated to her wordlessly. 'We've won. The company is safe. We have saved our son's future.'

Outside, the two disconsolately sat on the steps of the house.

"I don't know what's going on," protested Ajai Vir "So many guys dead, our factory burned down, and Dad says everything will be fine. I really don't understand it. But at least," he ended in satisfaction, "Prabal Kumar's finished."

Chris nodded. The politicians, the people, the press, all were unanimous that the villain of the tragedy was Prabal Kumar. Even if he was not convicted, since there was still no tangible proof that he was responsible for setting the fire, it would be a long time before he was released from jail. The government was certain to make an example out of him, on one pretext or another at least to divert attention away from their own failings. In any event, Prabal Kumar's career as a trade union leader and politician was over.

"Yep," Chris agreed somberly, picking up a pebble and tossing it to skip along the ground. "Wow, what a way to go. You know Ajai Vir," he confessed, turning to look at his friend, so different and yet so similar to him, "Indian politics really ain't no place for an American football player."

Some miles away, Sevak Chand sat in his vast office, with all the main newspapers lying scattered in front of him. His hunched figure, the bony vulpine head resting on its scrawny neck, peered at the photographs of the rows of covered bodies. The hooded eyes scanned the headlines, the comments, the reactions. Then satisfied, he pushed away the newspaper closest to him and leaned back.

His hands folded themselves over his stomach, those unfathomable eyes closed in thought. And then after a while when he had finished thinking, had examined the entire situation closely from every conceivable angle, when no one was in the office, when no one saw, the Minister smiled. And smiled. And smiled.